# The Plague

# The Plague

Nightcrawler, Book III

*John Reinhard Dizon*

Published 2016 by Creativia
Book design by Creativia (www.creativia.org)
Cover Design by Cover Mint

# Chapter One

Sabrina Brooks dreamed she was inside a dark, gloomy warehouse dressed in an armored ninja uniform. She was with a tall, powerfully-built man who staggered ahead of her as if he was drunk. She had a modified blower in her hand and held it against the man's shoulders as she prodded him through the darkness. Her senses were tingling, and her female instincts told her there was danger ahead. At length she heard faint sounds outside the warehouse, and by the approach she could tell they were unconcerned whether they were detected or not.

"Sergei!" a man's voice bellowed as three men barged through the front door. "Did you kill that little dog? We need to leave here before the police arrive!"

"Wait, Yuri," the second man pointed in Sabrina's direction. "There he is. He may have been wounded, look at him."

"Sergei, what has happened to you?" the leader called out. "Did you let that little scum of a man overcome you?"

"You know something, you've got a real smart mouth on you," Sabrina could not help herself.

The Chechens were armed with Smith and Wesson 500 revolvers which fired .50 caliber bullets. They loaded their weapons with full metal-jacketed rounds that would pierce hard targets only to explode when ruptured. The slugs tore through Sergei like a hot knife through butter and slammed into Sabrina's Teflon armor. She knew that if she took a double impact at any point on her armor, the bullets would tear through her body and kill her instantly. She raised her boot and shoved on Yuri's buttocks, launching him towards the hail of bullets as she dove for cover.

"Stop, you fools!" the third man yelled. "We've killed Sergei!"

"And we'll be next if we don't finish that little cretin!" the second man snarled. "Let's go finish him!"

At once they smelled a foul odor, and realized they were victims of the Nightcrawler's fabled chemical weaponry. They tried to hold their breaths but felt their throats and nostrils filling with a gluey mucus. They began gagging and spitting but could not draw breath, and felt their eyes closing as their eyelids became crusted. They tried to cry out to each other but could barely gasp. In desperation they began firing at the spot where the Nightcrawler had stood, hoping that a random shot found its mark before they were incapacitated.

Sabrina began backing away from the gunfire before a round hammered into her left chest. She turned away from the fusillade but caught a second bullet on her right wrist which caused her to drop the gas gun. She crouched to retrieve her weapon just as a third slug caught her on the side of her face.

She felt as if she was hammered with a baseball bat. The titanium steel reinforcement on her balaclava did not yield, but was driven into her face as if by a nail gun. She had been hit like this many times, and knew she had to go on the defensive and take stock of her surroundings. She saw the light of a window to her right, and knew she had to give them enough of a silhouette to allow them to blow the glass out. It was probably wire-reinforced glass, and she would have to pull this off in one move lest they realized they had her trapped.

"Agghhhh…agghhh…" Yuri croaked, pointing at her. At once a hail of bullets rained in her direction, and as the window exploded behind her she leaped for her life through the broken glass.

"Look!" she heard the voices of men outside the warehouse. Four SUVs had pulled up outside the building and had their headlights beaming upon the window where Sabrina appeared. "It's the Nightcrawler! Fire!"

At once there was a storm of bullets, and she felt herself exploding into nothingness…

"Hey. Hey!"

The sound of footsteps echoed closer to the room against the distant sound of hectic activity. A nurse rushed into the room and scowled at the visitor.

"She's moving around, kinda twitching. Maybe she's trying to wake up."

The nurse came over and checked Sabrina Brooks' vital signs, then inspected the readings on the monitors surrounding her hospital bed.

"She's just dreaming, Detective Wexford. I think the doctor explained it to you. It's definitely a good sign, it means her brain functions haven't closed down. Unfortunately it doesn't mean she's recovering from her coma."

"My gosh," he turned away so that the nurse could not see the tears welling in his eyes. "Doesn't anyone think it could be her trying to resurface? Maybe she's struggling in there, trying to wake up. Isn't there any way to help pull her up?"

"I assure you, Detective Wexford…"

"Hoyt."

"Hoyt, sir," the black girl warmed up. "She is getting the best care available. I don't want to make it sound like any of our patients receive any better care than others, but I've seen specialists and equipment brought into this facility that I've never seen before. Plus the fact that the Government has taken a special interest in this situation, rest assured that everyone is doing their best to make sure that Miss Brooks recovers."

He turned away and walked out of the room, angrily trying to regain his bearings. The bustling corridor was always full of personnel and visitors, but it was the black-suited men who irritated him most. They were in and out, appearing and disappearing like dark insects, leaving only when direct attention was paid to them. At first he was concerned that they might have been connected with the Russian Mob that wanted the Nightcrawler dead. After having a couple of them rousted he learned they were Government agents. It made him no less comfortable with their presence, and even less so when they got right up in his face.

"Detective Wexford?"

"Yeah?"

"I'm Kelly Stone with Homeland Security. I thought I might have a word."

Kelly was a solidly-built Oklahoman, about 5'11", 200 pounds, with a thick head of brown hair and dark, piercing eyes. He wore a classy blue suit, shirt and tie which gave him the mien of a Wall Street broker. It rankled Hoyt that these young urban professionals were being recruited as enforcers of this Administration's Constitution-shredding tactics, but even more so that this one was confronting him with impunity.

"Well, I'll tell you. I didn't get much sleep last night. I haven't been sleeping well since my fiancé went into a coma weeks ago. I'm getting ready to go to work at Police Plaza where I'm involved in a grandmaster chess match against the Russian Mob. I'll probably skip breakfast, which will put me in a worse mood than I'm in now."

"I'm really sorry for what's been going on here," Kelly did his best to read Hoyt's disposition. "My people thought it'd be a good idea for me to clear the air."

"So they decided to send up the kind of guy I'd want to throw a football around with."

"I'm sure you catch the same kind of heat from the lifers at your workplace."

"Let's get to it. What's on your mind."

"Look, we're just trying to get a foot in the door where the Nightcrawler's squaring off against the Russian Mob. You deal with those guys on a daily basis, you know they're invisible to the naked eye. All of their business is done overseas or within their own community. The fact they've been linked to the recent Chechen terror attacks is phenomenal. Not to mention the attempts to kill the Nightcrawler."

"I know you guys think Bree is going to give you a lead on the Nightcrawler," Hoyt grew testy. "Well, it's not happening. I'm her fiancé, I know every detail about her personal life. She spends – spent – up to twelve hours a day running her chemical company. On her days off she's with me. Look, I'm a New York City police detective, don't you think I'd have an inkling if she had any connection to the Nightcrawler? Do you think I'd risk my career covering up for her if she did? Just because they found her in a Nightcrawler-looking suit after she nearly got killed by Boko Haram doesn't make her the Nightcrawler."

"Well, he's obviously still out there, and she's in here, so that rules that out. Plus you're one of the few people who've seen the Nightcrawler, so you'd be the best one to know the difference. Hey, nobody in their right mind thinks Ms. Brooks is – or was - the Nightcrawler. There's people who just can't help but think she knows something about the Nightcrawler. There's the chemical weapons thing, as well as the fact she may have been an eyewitness to the Dariya Romanova murder at the Brooks campus. We also think the Nightcrawler escaped that explosion that killed the Boko Haram operatives and injured Ms. Brooks."

"You know, we pieced the whole thing together, you can pick up a copy of the closed case report downtown. Obviously Bree put on the costume to make Boko Haram think the Nightcrawler was guarding the campus. She was worried that the Russian Mob was going to try and leverage her company for information about the AIDS vaccine research. It looks like her intel was solid, because they murdered Dariya and kidnapped Bree. Maybe the Nightcrawler got involved, maybe he didn't. All we know is that Boko Haram got killed by one of their own bombs, and that we found a truckload of explosives outside their warehouse undoubtedly marked for a high-profile destination. We're seeing Bree as a victim here, not an accomplice."

"We're still trying to establish the connection between Boko Haram and the Russian Mob. Maybe the Chechen Mob was the go-between, maybe not."

"As far as we know, the Chechen Mob and the Mafiya has made the peace. That would restore the connection, don't you think?"

"My boss on Pennsylvania Avenue doesn't go on assumptions, Detective."

"Call me Hoyt, Kelly."

"Okay, Hoyt. This Nightcrawler has been going *mano a mano* with the Russian Mob over the last month, and he's got to know more about them than anyone outside of the Russian network. He's been harassing and interdicting their infrastructure, he's avoided every trap they've set for him, and he's been perfecting his own chemical arsenal. We can't even tell what he's using anymore."

"*We?*" Hoyt squinted. "All that's classified police information."

"*We* just rummage through garbage cans," Kelly smiled. "Relax, Big Brother hasn't tossed the Constitution into any of them just yet."

"Not just yet," Hoyt said pointedly.

"Oh, Hoyt, there you are, I thought you'd be around somewhere."

Both men were caught off-guard by the appearance of Rita Hunt. Bree's best friend was dressed in a dark power skirt suit that enhanced her hourglass figure. Her beautiful face was framed by her long chestnut hair, and her Kentuckian drawl was enough to cause any man's heart to flutter.

"Hey, Rita. This is Kelly Stone from Homeland Security."

"Well, uh, I was just leaving. Say, I'm just dying for a cup of coffee. You think you might want to show me where the cafeteria is? I'd be more than glad to buy you a cup."

"Nice try, flatfoot. I'm sure Bree wouldn't be happy to know I stood by while her buddy got hit on by one of you guys."

"I hope I'm not interrupting anything," Rita blushed. "Hoyt, why don't I come by later?"

"No, no," Kelly reached inside his jacket. "Miss Hunt, why don't I give you my card?"

"Give it to the fat lady at the desk on the way out," Hoyt took Rita's arm and ushered her away.

"You can call me at the White House," Kelly called after them.

"Persistent little cuss," Hoyt shook his head.

"I just stopped in to see Bree, and they told me you'd been by. Oh, she looks so pretty, those nurses make her up so wonderfully."

"Yeah, it's killing me," Hoyt's voice thickened.

"Are they still lurking around trying to talk to her?"

"Yeah, the damned Government. They're clutching for straws trying to catch the Nightcrawler. They think he can help them crack the Russian Mob."

"Hoyt, there's something I never told you," she looked into his eyes as they stopped at a window overlooking the pavilion outside Bellevue Hospital. "When I first met Bree, there was an incident. I'm sure you remember that time last year when the Mayor's partner's nephew had an altercation with the Nightcrawler."

"Yeah, it was all over the papers."

"Well, the girl that was being abused by the so-called victim was my niece."

"Did Bree – does Bree know that?"

"We went to see my niece after she was released from the hospital. We came after work in our dress clothes and that black guy nearly assaulted us. Bree put on something like what looked like that Nightcrawler costume and went back in there. The next day, that article came out in the papers. For a long time I had my suspicions, but after the Nightcrawler fell off the Statue of Liberty and that blimp in the New York harbor, I knew it wasn't her."

"Have you ever told anyone about this?" Hoyt searched her face.

"No, never, not 'til now."

"Let's keep it between us," he insisted. "If guys like Stone got hold of it, they'd pop open a fresh can of worms. It's all I can do to keep those vultures from perching on her bedpost."

"That's why I came to you. I just had to get it off my chest."

"Good," he smiled. "Uh, did Bree ever say anything to you about meeting the Nightcrawler, or knowing about him in any way?"

"No, never. We never discussed that day ever again. It was just one of those things you don't talk about in a friendship. We saw how the newspapers turned the incident into a public spectacle. I guess we both knew that they would've dragged Bree and my niece through the mud if they had the chance. Neither one of us considered the consequences of her going back there and calling him out. I'll tell you, though, if you'd been there you would've gone in yourself, even if you weren't a police officer. I would've gone in myself, but he would've beat the piss out of me."

"I'm glad you didn't. Things just had a way of working themselves out, didn't they?"

"Say, here comes Mr. Aeppli."

Hoyt shook hands with the silver-haired president of Brooks Chemical Company as Rita gave him a hug before taking her leave.

"I just thought I'd stop by and see how our girl was doing."

"Nothing new. Say, did you ever find out who was paying for all this?"

"It's like I said, she set up this so-called Brooks Foundation without my knowledge." Hoyt was always fascinated how the older man's cobalt eyes bored into their focal point like lasers. "All of a sudden we started getting these phone calls about how our funding was going to be covered after the Russians pulled out of the AIDS project. I was also told by the billing department at the hospital that Bree's expenses were being taken care of. It sounds like some off-shore deal. Every time I try to make inquiries I get tied up in some relay network in the Caribbean. I guess she had already planned for this day in advance."

"I just can't figure out why she never told you. She thinks of you like a father."

"She thinks of you like a future husband. I'd think you'd be her go-to guy."

"If I had any control over her, this would've never happened."

"Her father was my partner and my best friend," Jon looked out the window next to where they stood. "He would've wanted me to watch over her. Now look where we are."

"Let's quit beating ourselves up," Hoyt decided. "We've got to move on. We've got to get her up out of that bed. We can't give up on her. And you've got to keep her company ready for when she comes back."

"It's been rough sailing," Jon exhaled. "We ordered a lot of equipment we can't use, and some of the suppliers are balking because these were special orders. When the Russians pulled out, our Government pulled the plug on the whole project. We're getting lots of queries from private researchers, but no one's offering the kind of money we need to keep the ball rolling. Plus the whole thing's traumatized our workforce. You know how many of those gay guys were counting on our success."

"I know the feeling. I've been through three high-level debriefings so far. Homeland Security grilled me about the aborted chlorine bomb attack by Boko Haram at the Sberbank Rossii building on Wall Street. After that the Chief and the Captain put me through the wringer about Clyde Giroux and the corruption allegations against our team. Next Lieutenant Shreve calls me in for an interview with the Russian Security Service on their investigation of Alex Tretiak. In every meeting they made it sound like I masterminded the whole damned thing."

"We've all got our burdens to bear," Jon replied as he headed towards the exit. "Let's just hope we can help that little girl carry hers."

\* \* \*

Just a couple of miles away, a meeting was in progress at the Dagestani Dress Company in the Garment District of Manhattan. The people in attendance would also have a major impact in the life of Sabrina Brooks. They convened in a dusty room furnished with antiquated metal tables, chairs and cabinets that seemed a century removed from the glass and chrome splendor of the lower level showroom.

"It is a good thing that we are finally able to meet, praise Allah," the leader of the group opened the meeting. "As you both know, I am Colonel Boris Semenko of the Federal Security Service in Moscow. I am also a member of Tryzub, as are we all. We have been sent here to pick up where the Malkin triplets left off. Only our leaders in Makhachkala have modified our goals. Instead of destroying the Russian Mafiya, we will be working with them to carry out our terror campaign in bringing America to its knees. The Americans are already engaged in a crucial struggle against the Ebola epidemic. They will be entirely unprepared to defend themselves against what we are about to bring them."

"Have you brought the weapon?" the second man asked.

"The canisters are off-shore, waiting to be launched."

"Praise be to Allah," the woman said.

"My comrade, this is Cesaro Francium, a retired Captain of the GRU Spetsnaz of the Russian Army. He is a ranking member of the Tryzub Military Command in Makhachkala. He goes by the code name of Apollyon. He played a major role in the military campaigns in Grozny over the last decade as well as the Beslan operation in 2004. Let us just say that, when the name of Apollyon is mentioned in tradecraft, all who hear it know that death and destruction are not far behind."

"I'm pleased to know that I will be working with the best."

"And this is Chakra Khan, the leader of our cell unit in Nigeria. She goes by the code name of Black Diamond. She also holds rank in Boko Haram and has played a major role in their campaigns in Borno and Gwoza. The mention of the Black Diamond in Nigeria brings with it a portent of wholesale slaughter and mass annihilation."

"I'm sure Comrade Khan is just as familiar with your own exploits. The Colonel has masterminded the annexation of the Crimea and the ongoing guerilla war in the Ukraine, as well as the shoot-down of the Malaysian aircraft a short time back," Cesaro noted. "Now that we are all familiar with one another's penchant for mass destruction, let us proceed. How will we attend to the matters at hand?"

"The mission is twofold. As we know, Homeland Security is still investigating the deaths of the Malkin triplets. It is giving our people time to cover their tracks. The Federal Security Service has taken over the inquiry concerning Alexander Malkin, so that matter is fairly well closed. We have linked Grigori Malkin to the Russian Mob, so that is leading the NYPD into a dead end. The death of Dariya Malkin is still being investigated as a homicide, making her a victim rather than a suspect. It facilitates our move into position as the new leaders of the American Tryzub."

"How are we going to repair the bridge between us and the Mafiya?" Cesaro asked.

"It has already been take care of in Moscow. Our connections with the Chechen Mob acted as intercessors. In exchange for a forty percent commission, the Mafiya will provide us full support in blackmailing the Government for one hundred million dollars ransom. Within forty-eight hours, we will be sending them samples of the mutated Ebola virus our scientists have developed. We will then exchange the canisters of EVDIII in exchange for the ransom money. If they refuse, the canisters will be used in attacks on the people of New York City. It will cause paralysis throughout the financial networks of the nations of the world. From there it will be easier to blackmail other nations in future endeavors."

"It is a lofty goal," Cesaro concurred. "Let us hope we are equal to the task."

"The secondary objective will be to eliminate the Nightcrawler once and for all. This masked vigilante has been conducting raids against our Mafiya colleagues ever since our Boko Haram assassins were killed a few weeks ago. Apparently the Nightcrawler established the connection between the Mafiya and Boko Haram. This is a well-trained, elusive and cunning adversary who is not only well-informed but well-equipped with unique and highly effective equipment. At first he was using what seemed a modified form of our own Kolokol-1, but now it seems he has a derivative which is twice as effective and easier to produce."

"May I ask where we are getting all this information?" Chakra inquired.

"Ironically, the deaths of the Malkins opened up a whole new dialogue between the Security Service, Homeland Security and the NYPD. They are now freely trading information in order to shut down the Chechen Mob and the Mafiya in New York City. Unknown to them, we have double agents in both the hierarchy and middle management throughout the Security Service. All of their information is placed on our tables on a silver platter."

They shared a hearty laugh.

"The downside is that we are receiving most troubling information on the Nightcrawler, and it tells us more about what we do not know about him," Boris frowned. "He has been one step ahead of us in every phase of the game. We have every reason to believe that he has informers inside the Russian community. We also believe he has connections to the business community, the scientific community and law enforcement. We believe that he has a contact within the Brooks Chemical Company, possibly with its CEO. However, Sabrina Brooks suffered injuries which put her in a coma during the attack against Boko Haram. We have agents watching her hospital room, awaiting word of her recovery so we may gain further information from her. That, unfortunately, may not happen for some time to come. Instead we have decided to kill the Nightcrawler and remove this stumbling block from our path to success."

"How was Brooks involved in the attack on Boko Haram?" Cesaro wondered.

"This is where it gets murky. The NYPD and Homeland Security are also waiting to debrief Ms. Brooks for the same reason. The general consensus is that the Nightcrawler learned about a plan by Boko Haram to kidnap Ms. Brooks. For what reason we do not know. Apparently the gambit was to dress Ms. Brooks as the Nightcrawler and use Dariya Malkin as bait. The Boko Haram agents staged a raid on the Brooks Chemical complex, and Dariya had no choice but to defend Brooks. Boko Haram had no knowledge of Dariya being part of Tryzub, and killed her in the skirmish. They then took Brooks back to their waterfront hideout, where the Nightcrawler overtook them. There was an explosion that killed the agents and incapacitated Brooks. Somehow the Nightcrawler escaped."

"From your words, it seems that the Nightcrawler may have stood by and watch our agents kill Malkin and kidnap Brooks in order to trail our people to their hideout," Chakra pointed out. "That seems somewhat ruthless for a crimefighter."

"This Nightcrawler is a complex and somewhat unstable individual," Boris concurred. "Homeland Security considers him an armed and extremely dangerous person of interest, as do the FBI and the NYPD. The only reason he has not made Ten Most Wanted is because keeping him in play is putting our Mafiya colleagues out of business. We believe that even the American President is given progress reports on Nightcrawler activity. By killing this man, we will prove to the Americans that the Tryzub is invincible. It will make our hand all the more stronger when we present the Americans with our demands."

"Enough talk," Cesaro grunted. "Present us with your plan so we may put it into action."

"Gladly," Boris smiled. "Let us begin."

\* \* \*

Later that day, another plan of action was being implemented by the NYPD.

Hoyt Wexford had been summoned to another upper echelon meeting at Police Plaza in Lower Manhattan at 1100. Captain Tyrone Willard was there along with Lieutenant Detective Dwight Shreve and three other faces he was familiar with during his short time at the NYPD law enforcement hub. They all shook hands in the spacious conference room before the session began.

"As you know, there is an ongoing investigation of this individual known as the Nightcrawler," Willard opened the dissertation, displaying a Power Point screen shot of blurry images depicting a black-garbed figure. "There are units from Homeland Security and the FBI here in the Big Apple snooping around for leads on the case, and most of them just happen to be groping our butts on a daily basis. As you can imagine, Commissioner Jordan, Chief Madden and I have been made extremely uncomfortable. You gentlemen are being deputized to make sure that this groping comes to an end."

"I guess they haven't sent too many female agents up from D.C.," Donald Conroy chuckled.

"That may be why you don't see a smile on my face," Willard growled. "As you may or may not know, Detective Wexford is one of the few people we know of who has seen this Nightcrawler at close range, and has even engaged in conversation with this individual. This is why Wexford is being assigned to lead this four-man task force."

"Not to step on the young detective's toes, but to my knowledge, he hasn't been here in Police Plaza long enough to shop for winter clothing," Bob Methot spoke up. "Don't you think you should have someone leading the pack who won't need to be asking for directions?"

"Right now, your best move is going to be moving in the direction of the Russian Mob," Shreve spoke up. "Hoyt's got more than enough experience dealing with those guys."

"I'm just here to get the job done," Hoyt interjected. "I've got no problem with moving over and letting someone else drive. If they want me to be the one to put the report on the teacher's desk, so be it."

"I'll go along with that," Jerry Loverdi offered. "I'm a football kind of guy. You get a helluva lot more done as a team as opposed to one guy trying to run the ball on his own."

"Okay, so we've settled that. Let's move on," Willard continued. "Apparently the Nightcrawler has declared war against the Russian Mob in the Brighton Beach area of Brooklyn. This has been an ongoing campaign over the last few months, and it's not only been an embarrassment to this Department but has cost the Mafiya some serious money. They have escalated their efforts to eliminate the Nightcrawler, and we're seeing weapons moving into Brighton on an unprecedented scale."

"I read the files," Methot stroked his chin. "The last time they laid a trap for this guy, they used armor-piercing rounds and couldn't put him down."

"Chief, I've got a theory of my own," Hoyt was hesitant. "Suppose they actually took the Nightcrawler out and someone stepped up to take his place? Suppose there's more than one Nightcrawler? After all, how could anyone keep surviving these attacks and keep coming back for more?"

"The think tankers in Washington passed that idea along," Willard nodded. "It's a possibility we're not ruling out. Slight, but not out of the question. The problem with that theory is that there would be more to lose by announcing a Nightcrawler Army that has dedicated itself to wiping out the Russian Mob. One man acting alone is a nuisance that can be eliminated in the right place and time. More than one Nightcrawler would be a nightmare."

"I know this has to be stressful for Hoyt, and my condolences to him over Sabrina Brooks' condition. Everyone in the Department is praying for her speedy recovery," Jerry, a swarthy Italian, spoke up. "I know we have people looking to interview her about her encounter with the Nightcrawler and Boko Haram. I just think we're looking in the wrong direction. We know there are Boko Haram cells in East Harlem. Why aren't we posting units on their doorstep to see what they're gonna do next?"

"Our Upper Manhattan precincts are on them like flies on a turd," Willard made them chuckle. "We have no doubt that they want a piece of the Nightcrawler too. Only the Harlem Boko Haram is playing the race card, trying to gain some political leverage. If they make a move on the Nightcrawler, it'll be at the Mafiya's behest. Look, I don't like having detectives waiting for Sabrina to get out of bed any more than anyone else. Hoyt knows it too. Only she's the last one we know besides the Mafiya who's seen this guy. We're grasping for straws, gentlemen, and our Commissioner and our Chief of Police can't afford to be perceived as grasping for straws. You guys are gonna change the game for us."

"Hey, I'm a team player, one for all and all for one," Donald, a curly blond Irishman, spoke up. "I hate to point out the fact that Clyde Giroux's team caused lots of Russians to put up 'Not Welcome' signs all over Brighton. When they see Hoyt coming back, it may cause lots of hard guys to get a hard-on for us."

"This is where you want to put on your public relations caps and build us some collateral. Go in there as liberators, not as conquerors. We're not going in there to take the streets back from the Mafiya. We're in there to free them from the Russian Mob. Our hunch is that if you find people who are chafing under the yoke, chances are you may find someone who's leaking information to someone who knows the Nightcrawler."

"Not for nothing, but what precautions should we be taking against the plague?" Methot asked.

"Put on gloves and a mask if it makes you feel warm and fuzzy," Shreve shot back. "Half the people on Wall Street are wearing them. I'll bet my bottom dollar it's the other half that's still making money in the crisis economy."

"Yeah, and I hope you're making sure my family's still getting the checks."

"Hey, you get your hazard pay like everyone else. You also got the creds, Bob. You think the street's too dangerous, put in papers for a desk job."

"Yeah, yeah," Methot waved him off.

"You guys went to the Ebola seminar just like everyone else," Willard emphasized. "Keep everyone outside your airspace. Don't make physical contact unless absolutely necessary. Have your gloves and mask in your pockets at all times if contact is unavoidable. If you start feeling like you have symptoms of any kind, head to an emergency clinic immediately. There's lots of serums out there that have proved successful in treating the disease. Don't be a hero. If you feel a headache coming on, drop everything and head for the nearest clinic. Your life may depend on it."

"Hey, Dwight, now that makes me feel warm and fuzzy," Donald quipped.

"You know, that could be an angle," Jerry proffered. "Not to sound cold-blooded, but if we encourage some of the down-and-outers to come in for examinations, it might make us look more like good-will ambassadors than anything."

"One thing I've learned about the Russian people is that they loathe bull-shitters," Hoyt disagreed. "Let's face it, they came over here from a land of lies and deception and found out that it's the same all over. They're gonna see who we are the minute we come through the door. All I'm gonna be able to do is to go back there and say I wanna make things right. I can't take back what Clyde Giroux and Alexander Tretiak did, but I can show them that all cops aren't the same."

"One thing I cannot overemphasize is that you guys are not in there to jack with the Russian Mob," Willard insisted. "You are the Nightcrawler Task Force. We are trying to pick up on the informers that are supplying our suspect with his information. If we can stop the Nightcrawler, we will put an end to the Mafiya's demand for heavy weaponry. This is going to create a glut in the market, and they'll be trying to dump their surplus to recoup their investments. This is where the ATF steps in and takes down their hierarchy on Federal weapons charges. It's a win-win situation, guys. Retire the Nightcrawler, constipate the Russian Mob, and we'll have the top Mafiya dogs in the kennel at Attica by Christmastime."

"I say we head on over to Manitoba's to scratch out a game plan," Methot exhorted his teammates as they left the conference room shortly afterwards. "Couple of beers, some shots of JD and chili cheese fries can do wonders to inspire men's souls,"

"I agree," Hoyt chimed in. "We do our partying before we cross the bridge. We don't do what Clyde did. We don't want to look as bad as the Russian vors."

"That kinda rhymes with Russian whores," Jerry grinned. "Definitely don't wanna look that bad."

And so the new Nightcrawler Task Force set out along their path which would change the destiny of New York City forever.

# Chapter Two

Sabrina dreamed of a time when she had gone to a church picnic with her parents on a sunny afternoon. They were there for less than an hour when a bruised Sabrina was escorted back to her parents by one of the female elders. Mrs. Brooks, a beautiful woman with long auburn hair that her daughter inherited, inspected Sabrina's bruise as her husband asked what had happened. The second-grader explained that she had beaten the boys in a race, then went undefeated in a game of King of the Hill. They began teasing her as a tomboy until she won a fight against the biggest of the boys.

"Daddy, are you ashamed of me because I'm not a boy?" she was forlorn.

"No, honey, I'm more proud of you than anything else in this world," he took her in his arms and hugged her close before holding her at arms' length, gazing into her eyes. "Now listen to me. You are just the way God wanted you to be when He sent you to us. You're God's gift to me and your Mommy. You're perfect just the way you are, and you should always think of yourself that way. There's only one Sabrina Brooks. No one else can ever be like you. You just be the best you can be, don't try to be like anyone else. If you do, you're just going to be an imitation. You just be you, and everyone'll love you for the wonderful girl you are."

"Amen," Sabrina's mother put her arms around her daughter's waist from behind and snuggled her neck. "Now go on and play with the other girls. You don't have to prove anything to anyone. God doesn't want you getting in fights. You just be sweet as you are."

"Okay, Mommy."

*You're so beautiful...so beautiful...*

"Mr. Wexford?"

Hoyt looked around and saw a six-foot, three hundred pound black woman in a nurse's uniform standing behind her. She was dark as pitch, with her hair wound tightly in a bun at the back of her massive head. He could not help but think she would have given a healthy Sabrina a serious run for her money.

"My name is Nurse Ratched, Minnie Ratched. I've been appointed as Ms. Brooks' personal caretaker. I'm working directly under Dr. Eric Schumann, who has been assigned as Ms. Brooks' personal physician by her benefactors at the Brooks Foundation."

"Ah, yes, the Ring Cycle," Hoyt smirked. "Is there a supervisor I could talk to?"

"You looking at her. I'm the supervisor, manager, whatever I gots to be. I reports to Dr. Schumann, there is no go-between."

"So how is it that you people get appointed without any advance notice, no one having any say in the matter? Where's that little nurse, Shakeera? Does Jon Aeppli know about this?"

"Shakeera was relieved, by me. I'm not sure what kind of a problem you're having here."

"Shakeera was working for Bellevue, wasn't she? How did they approve you taking her place without discharging Sabrina from the hospital?"

"Mr. Wexford…"

"Hoyt."

"It's none of my business, and I don't want to make it mine. I can only assume that she's being kept here so the Government can keep an eye out for her."

"More than likely to keep an eye *on* her," Hoyt sneered. "What are your credentials? How do I know you're not working for Homeland Security?"

"Mr. Wexford, you need to do your detective work with the Brooks Foundation. I have enough on my plate taking care of this comatose woman than worrying about living up to your expectations."

"All right, well, how about me paying a visit to this Dr. Schumann?"

"Dr. Schumann easy enough to find. He just rented a suite overlooking Central Park. He came up here from Austin, Texas to oversee Ms. Brooks' treatment and rehabilitation."

Hoyt caught sight of Jon Aeppli arriving for his daily visit and took leave of Nurse Ratched, who was positioning Sabrina for a sponge bath.

"Jon," he greeted him. "You know anything about this, this Nurse Ratched? Sounds like that character from *One Flew Over The Cuckoo's Nest*."

"Did you mention that to her?"

"No."

"Good. She doesn't like it."

"So you were up here earlier?"

"I had the same reaction as you probably did. I called up some old connections in Texas and got the lowdown on Dr. Schumann. He's one of the leading experts in the treatment of myxedema coma patients."

"I'm still kinda fuzzy on all that. They explained that it was a result of Sabrina's collarbone having been fractured by the bomb blast. It damaged her thyroid gland and caused thyroiditis to set in, which led to hypothyroidism that put her in a coma."

"Well, my theory is that the original shock from the blast was what put her in a coma, and the hypothyroidism is what they're dealing with now. Be that as it may, I made some calls and arranged for you to go up and have a chat with Schumann."

"Mr. Aeppli, you are da man!" Hoyt mimicked a ghetto accent, patting Jon's shoulder. "No beating around the bush for you, go straight to the heart of the matter."

"It's too bad you've alienated all of Homeland Security's lap dogs up here. You might've got one of them to do some digging around the Brooks Foundation."

"I don't like Feds, Jon. I kinda got allergic to them since I moved up to Police Plaza. They have a way of swiping other people's work and taking credit for it. Still... say, wait. I got an idea."

"And what's that?"

"That snoop dog Kelly Stone had an eye on Bree's friend Rita. Maybe I can get Rita to play nice with him and get him to take a look."

"Rita's a nice girl, she's one of Bree's church friends," Jon stared at him. "I don't think it's a good idea."

"Hey, she's Bree's best friend," Hoyt insisted. "I'm not talking about her sleeping with the bastard. I'm just thinking she can let him take her to dinner or something. Don't worry, those gals from Warren County can take care of themselves. That Fed doesn't have anything up his sleeve that Kentucky woman can't handle."

"Good. Say, I didn't get to ask you yesterday. Anything on the other guy?"

"Hah," Hoyt scoffed. "I just got appointed team lead of a four-man unit assigned to track him down. Talk about mixing business with pleasure."

"So why aren't they letting down their guard here at the hospital?"

"It's like I said. They don't remotely suspect Bree of being the Nightcrawler. They just think she's been involved with him somehow. I just don't see how he could be using the same type of chemical weapons Bree has. Are you sure there's no one at the plant who Bree might have brought in to keep the operation going if anything happened to her?"

"I've been asking you the same thing. Whoever this guy is has extensive athletic and martial arts training to be doing what he's doing. Have you checked out everybody at the police academy she had contact with when she was there?"

"I'm getting stretched kinda thin these days, Jon. There's still a couple of names on my list who could fit the bill. Look, let's just both keep our eyes open, we're sure to spot something. This guy didn't just spring up from nowhere and decide to become the perfect Nightcrawler knockoff. Bree must have had him waiting for the day when she was put out of action. It just seems impossible that she could've set it up without either of us knowing."

"If he gets caught, obviously it'd take the heat off Bree, but I'd hate to see them throw the book at the guy. Other than that, my biggest hope is that he doesn't get himself killed."

"You and me both, Jon," Hoyt exhaled tautly. "You and me both."

* * *

Despite the fear spread by the Ebola plague through the streets of New York, the people of East Harlem came out in full force on this day. They first held a demonstration against alleged police brutality at the 40th Precinct of Mott Haven. They next marched to 137th Street and Lenox Avenue where a scaffold had been erected outside the Boko Haram Mosque storefront. Upon it were seated the elders of the mosque along with a special guest speaker who was determined to turn East Harlem politics asunder.

"People of Harlem! It is time for us to stand strong and united as proud black Americans who demand fair and equal treatment!" the woman began. Donna Summer was an athletically-built African standing over six feet tall, her hair ironed and bleached blonde as that of a white woman. Male blacks found her extremely attractive and were just as mesmerized by her looks as by her rich voice and her captivating presence.

"We will no longer stand by and watch our young black men be targeted by the New York City Police Department. We will no longer remain silent as our husbands and children are beaten, strangled and shot down on the city streets by the police. We call upon all of our neighbors in this community to join our church, surrender their lives to Allah and unite in the struggle against racism and genocide against black people across America!"

The blacks screamed and yelled, shaking their fists in the air as Donna's words stirred them into a frenzy. The police had endured abuse and great provocation in dealing with the mob at Alexander Avenue and were loath to rejoin the fray just blocks away. Nevertheless they did their duty is ensuring that the crowd did not obstruct traffic or endanger lives and property in the area. The throng misconstrued their efforts as a ploy to disperse the gathering and began harassing the police anew. The Black Muslims on the platform picked up on the altercations and fanned the flames ever higher with their vitriol.

"See how the infidels have recruited black traitors to wear their uniforms and persecute their own people!" Donna pointed at the black officers in their riot gear. "It is the same thing we see overseas, where the tyrants and murderers in Nigeria and throughout Mother Africa hire black men to kill, steal and destroy in their own communities! My brothers and sisters, Boko Haram is no longer a political party or a military organization! I hereby declare Boko Haram our religion, our philosophy, our way of life! Join Boko Haram and become one of us, proud Black Muslims wishing to spread the peace, joy and happiness of Allah throughout all of Harlem! We will bring the love and joy of Islam to all of New York and to the entire world!"

The police found themselves to be the targets of rocks and bottles as the blacks began pelting them from safe distances. The 137th Street Gang, which had been working with Boko Haram in developing a highly profitable drug network, began passing out Molotov cocktails and small-caliber guns for use against the police. The police began chasing after some of the agitators but dared not break rank lest they be dragged apart and overwhelmed. Eventually reinforcements arrived so that the officers were able to arrest their assailants and herd them into waiting police trucks. The blacks grew angrier but realized they were in an unwinnable fight.

"We have done well, Sister Donna," one of the elders praised her after the mosque leaders retreated into their sanctuary. "You are indeed a talented and motivational speaker, Allah be praised. It is time for us to introduce you to one of our own who will join you in bringing the infidels to their knees."

"It is my great pleasure, Sister Donna. Allah be praised."

Philemon Rubidium was what the other kids in East Harlem called a 'big-head nigger'. He reminded folks of the black ants in the cartoons, with the great oval skulls and the eyes that seemed to start on the sides of their heads. He was a tall man, which made his large head stick out above the crowd. He avoided people as a matter of habit, favoring the company of books and enjoying the comfort of his solitude. When the Black Muslims began recruiting in his East Harlem neighborhood, he found a place where he would be accepted for his intellect rather than judged by his odd appearance. He joined Islam, then became a minister and began speaking regularly at the 137th Street mosque. People were impressed by his eloquence, and soon Philemon was one of their most popular ministers.

"Let me introduce another of our dearest friends and major supporters," the elder beckoned towards a hulking black-clad man with a shaven head and goatee. "This is Kamala Brown. He is a leader of the 137th Street Crew, a prestigious group in our community. He has supported our mosque in countless ways over the past months and is considered an invaluable member of our infrastructure."

"I bring glad tidings from the king of kings, the Great Caliph of the Islamic State," Donna announced. "He has personally sent his blessings to our brothers in Dagestan, the jihadists of the Tryzub. They, in turn, have joined forces with the Muslim conquerors of Nigeria, Boko Haram. The world watches in terror as the Islamic takeover of the entire planet takes place before its eyes. Now is the time for us to unleash the plague foretold in the Koran against the nations of the infidels. Muslim scientists have developed a strain of Ebola that is without cure or remedy. We are prepared to demand one hundred million dollars from the American government in exchange for the formula. If our demands are not meant, it is up to us to strike the final blow against the Great Satan of America."

"What—what are you saying?" the elders gasped in shock. "Islam is a religion of peace. You cannot bring this terrible plague against the people of New York. There are three million black people living in New York City. You cannot bring this devastation against our brothers and sisters. If you do not desist we will be obliged to notify the authorities."

"Fools! Must I kill them all!" Donna raged. "Kill the Uncle Tom backsliders!"

At once Kamala produced a Glock-17 and began pouring fire upon the elders. The six clergymen realized that Donna had made a deal with the 137th Street Gang well before this meeting had been scheduled. They tried to rush for the exit but were soon drowning in their own blood.

"I can fix this! I can fix this!" Philemon cried out, his large eyes bulging in terror. "I will say that the elders resigned and left the city to bring the message of Allah to the nations of Africa. I'll say it was arranged so that Sister Donna was anointed as the new minister of Boko Haram Mosque. You leave it to me, and no one will know this ever happened."

"Let me tell you, nigger, if anyone finds out about this, I will perform a miracle in the name of Allah," Kamala waved his pistol in Philemon's face.

"Pray tell, my brother," Philemon shook with fright.

"I will make your big nigger head disappear up your skinny ass!" Kamala snorted, whipping out his cell phone. "Now start dragging these niggers out into the hallway so I can have my men get rid of them."

"We shall not call our brothers niggers," Donna insisted. "It is an offense to Allah, who made the black race superior to all mankind."

"You call it any way you want, my fine black sister," Kamala grinned before stepping away to take the phone call. "Just call me when they get to splitting that one hundred million."

Philemon shivered as four black men arrived ten minutes later with boxes of king-size garbage bags and small hacksaws.

"Don't you—have body bags for this kind of thing?"

"Homes, do you think we gonna carry six bodies outta here in broad daylight?" Kamala was derisive. "Get yourself a bag and a blade and give the brothers a hand."

"I—I don't think I can."

"Who gonna do the job for you, Donna? Now you put some plastic over them street clothes and get to work or we be chopping you up next!"

* * *

Later that afternoon Hoyt Wexford took the ride uptown to meet with Dr. Eric Schumann. The physician had a suite at the prestigious Empire Hotel at West 63<sup>rd</sup> Street and Broadway. It afforded him a sweeping view of Central Park just a couple of blocks away.

"How good it is to meet you, Detective Wexford," the men shook hands after Schumann bade Hoyt entry into his suite.

"My pleasure, Dr. Schumann."

The doctor was a tall, well-built man with his long brown hair tied back in a ponytail, something that Hoyt did not like. He had deep blue eyes and a pale golden tan which suggested summer weekends spent on the tennis court. He could easily see Schumann as the thinking member on a team with Kelly Stone.

"I heard that you and Jon Aeppli have been stopping by to visit Ms. Brooks daily," Schumann opened the meeting as they sat in the office area where the hotel had supplied him with a desk and cabinets. "I think that is a very important factor that may contribute to her recovery."

"How so?"

"I think of my patients as being trapped beneath the ice on a lake, swimming around trying to find a place to resurface," he spoke with a clipped German accent. "They seek light, sound and movement, anything that can help their consciousness reconnect their body with the real world. I personally believe there are other things involved. Are you a spiritual person, Detective?"

"No more or less than the next person, I guess."

"I tend towards Carl Jung's philosophy as respects the supernatural realm, though I would stop short of consulting psychics. I would not rule out the possibility of the patient being aware of her environment despite being unable to perceive it with her senses."

"Perceive it or not, we need to get her back to the land of the living. How're we coming with that?"

"To understand what we're dealing with here, it's helpful for one to have basic knowledge about how such things work," Schumann said gently. "The nerve cells in the brainstem are responsible for maintaining a waking state. Damage to these nerves can be caused by an explosion resulting in a severe concussion. This could be compounding the problem we're facing with what we think may be hypothyroidism."

"Right now you're still in the guessing stage, you don't know."

"This is why I mentioned Jung. The brain is a very complicated and delicate organ, perhaps the most unique in our universe. It can be affected by direct impact, indirect trauma, and conditions perceived by the mind itself."

"So you think there are psychological factors involved."

"Consider this, Detective Wexford. Our Sabrina is a fighter and a winner. She's the chief executive officer of a successful chemical company. She's also in extraordinary physical condition, a remarkable feat in itself considering the rigors of her professional life. We would assume her entire being is struggling to emerge from this comatose state, yet it is not happening. Nurse Ratched got reports from Nurse Smith – Shakeera – that Sabrina was showing signs of cognitive recovery. They said you were there when she was twitching, perhaps as the result of a dream."

"Yeah, yeah," Hoyt averted his gaze, wiping his eyes.

"I'm sorry, Detective. Would you like a glass of water?"

"No, I'm okay. Go on."

"This adds a third dimension to our problem. We must consider the fact that Sabrina is somehow aware of the police presence outside her room. Not you, Detective, but the many others who wish to have a word with her once she re-covers. Nurse Ratched tells me there are New York Police detectives, FBI agents and even Homeland Security officers roaming the halls. I have cursory informa-tion surrounding the events leading to Sabrina's accident. Nor am I interested in acquiring more than necessary. Be that as it may, it still leads me believe that Sabrina may be trying to protect someone by lingering in this vegetative state."

"Nightcrawler," Hoyt cupped his forehead. "Damned Nightcrawler."

"Pardon?"

"Okay, look, you're her doctor, right? She has a patient-doctor privilege ac-cording to law, isn't that right? Even if you get information from a third-party source like me."

"That is correct, Detective. And even if it were not the case, my own core values would keep me from betraying the confidence of a patient on principle."

"I'm pretty sure she's had contact with the Nightcrawler, the masked vig-ilante."

"Yes, I am quite aware of who he is. His name shows up on *Entertainment Tonight* as much as it does on *Good Morning America*."

"That's why those vultures are out there. Look, is there any way you could file a restraining order to get them out of there?"

"Such a thing would have to be done by the immediate family, a loved one, a business partner, or some confidant with whom she has a close relationship. It is simply out of the question for a member of the hospital staff or a provider such as myself due to the legal implications. If we could bar the police for reasons of harassment, it could make us liable if a perpetrator were able to slip through their fingers and commit another crime. What about Jon Aeppli, or perhaps Rita Hunt?"

"Jon's trying to keep her business afloat. If he made waves with the Feds, they might retaliate by rejecting his bid for the Ebola research project. Rita…nah, no way. Rita's just not that kind of girl. She's innocent in a wholesome kind of way. I couldn't ask her to get involved in a mess like that."

"Have you asked her?"

"I'm not going to, Doc…excuse me, Doctor Schumann." Hoyt perceived that this fellow was into prestige and would continue calling him Detective in exchange for the reciprocity. His way of conveying informality was by calling Sabrina by her first name. "If Sabrina ever found out she's be extremely annoyed with me. Besides, you don't know the Feds. They're liable to start leaning on her in retaliation. I'd never put Rita through that."

"Since we're being candid with one another, Detective, is it possible your protective feelings for Rita run a bit deeper than that? She is a beautiful woman, we know."

"Hey, what's up with that?" Hoyt flared. "She's my fiancé's best friend. I love Rita like a sister. If anybody ever made a move on her…"

"Good. Now we've eliminated any ulterior motives on your part. This is the part where you go to Rita and explain how important her help will be. Let us consider the Ebola outbreak. These agents are out on the field not wearing masks, gloves or other protective gear. They may easily be carrying the Ebola virus and possibly transmitting them to the personnel in this facility. Sabrina, as a chemical engineer, is well aware of the risks and may be shutting herself down to protect herself from exposure."

"So where are you taking this? Are you saying I could be bringing the plague in to her?"

"Highly unlikely. If you felt the symptoms you wouldn't come anywhere near here. Neither would Nurse Ratched or Nurse Smith. However, the Federal agents may not exhibit such restraint."

"I just can't do this," Hoyt slumped in his seat.

"Consider the option, and what's at stake," Schumann advised. "Sabrina's well-bring and recovery may depend on it."

* * *

"Hey, give me her phone number, maybe I can talk her into it over a candlelight dinner."

"Yeah, don't hold your breath."

Bob Methot had been waiting downstairs in the lobby nursing a drink while waiting for Hoyt. They cruised along in Bob's Jaguar heading back downtown as Hoyt told him about his visit with Schumann. Hoyt considered how unique the relationship between police officers could be. The two men only had a nodding acquaintance with one another over the past months. Now they knew almost everything about one another after being teamed together for a couple of weeks.

Methot was known as a gunslinger, a man without fear who was considered the worst and best of partners a cop could have. Bob could drag you in over your head in a moment's notice. Yet he was the best man on the force to have at your back in a jam. Three of his ex-partners were retired and one was six feet under. Hoyt considered the possibilities and decided that he was not going to end up on either list.

"I've been holding my breath for several weeks now," Bob nodded out the window as they cruised down Broadway. A quarter of the people walking along the bustling sidewalks wore paper masks. It eerily resembled the scene after 9/11 almost two decades ago. "Did you hear the one about IBM hustling people to donate their available PC space to fight Ebola?"

"How's that work?" Hoyt sipped his coffee.

"You download an app, and IBM can use your unused capacity to handle tasks they can upload into their databases. With the millions of computers around the world, it gives them a distributed computing ability that equals a supercomputer. It's like each computer is solving a fragment of a super-puzzle that IBM is working out. Think about it."

"Yeah, sounds like a plan."

"Consider the downside," Bob reached for his coffee on his car tray. "Suppose the Russian Mob latched onto the idea and began working on a computer virus? They could have networks across Russia, the USA and wherever else they have influence. They infect some bank and steal millions of dollars. As soon as the bank figures it out, the Russkies are already working on another one."

"I think the hacker networks are ahead of you on that one. Tell you one thing, though. I'm sure glad you're working on our side of the fence. You got one devious mind."

"I've had my offers," Bob chuckled.

As they passed Columbus Circle, they went bumper-to-bumper alongside an office building undergoing construction. It was wedged in next to a parking garage whose ramps intersected the flow of pedestrians on the sidewalk. They spotted a black car in a no parking area on the edge of the exit lane. Traffic was so heavy that no one paid mind until, at once, a body dropped from the sky and shattered the car windshield.

"Holy crap!" Bob hit the brakes. Hoyt rolled down the passenger window and saw four men in black approaching the car with satchels in hand. They stopped short in front of the vehicle, staring in shock as if uncertain of what to do. Hoyt took out his badge as he exited the car, causing three of the men to race back into the garage. The fourth man darted southward in the direction of Times Square.

"Bob, call for backup! I'll take care of the girl!" Hoyt was frantic. "Somebody call an ambulance!"

A crowd gathered to stare at the spectacle as Bob rushed from the Jaguar with his badge and pistol drawn. The female figure had long red hair that covered her face, her dark jumpsuit concealing any injuries or lacerations. Her weight had caved in the windshield as she laid motionless on the dashboard.

"Good idea," Bob ran off in pursuit of the men in black.

"Bob! Wait up!" Hoyt yelled. His cry fell upon deaf ears, forcing him to draw his own Glock-17 and run after Bob.

Methot was in excellent shape and had already made his way halfway up the ramp to the second level. Hoyt ran as fast as he could but was too late to engage in the resulting gunfire. He heard women and screaming and men yelling as shots were exchanged. Hoyt dropped into a crouch and assumed a triangular stance, leading with his weapon as he wheeled around the pillar supporting the ramp. He spotted a perpetrator sitting against a concrete wall overlooking Broadway, his eyes gazing blankly into space. His brains were splattered on the surface behind him.

"Bob!" Hoyt cried out as he heard another fusillade ringing out on the third level. There was more screaming and shouting and the sound of running feet. Hoyt led with his Glock barrel, pivoting around the dividing wall before charging up the ramp. He reached the third level to discover another fallen gunman sprawled face-first onto the pavement. His weapon and his satchel had not fallen far from his lifeless hands.

He could hear the sound of sirens below, boosting his confidence as he continued his race up the ramp in search of Bob. Once again he heard the echoing of automatic fire and ran ahead in a crouch, his eyes darting about for signs of the altercation. By now the pedestrians had vacated the area, and Hoyt could see Bob standing by the far wall. His pistol dangled from his hand as he gasped for breath, standing between Hoyt and a fallen perpetrator. Hoyt could see the man lying on the ground, blood flowing from his forehead into a spreading pool around his torn skull.

"Damn, I've had my exercise for the day," Bob grinned, wiping the sweat from his brow as he holstered his weapon. "Too bad we're gonna be up to our butts in paperwork for the rest of the afternoon. I could sure use a couple of beers at Manitoba's."

"You just killed three men," Hoyt mumbled, sheathing his own Glock. "You could've been one of them. Are you okay?"

"Sure, kid. You think I just started this job last week?" Bob chuckled, patting Hoyt on the back as NYPD officers came racing toward them with revolvers at the ready. "Let's get back downstairs and let the boys in blue do their job."

"Police officers," Hoyt held his badge out as officers fanned out with guns pointed at them. "We're plainclothes detectives. We intercepted them during a robbery in progress."

One of the officers recognized Bob, and they all holstered their weapons as they began investigating the scene.

"Are you guys okay?" a cop walked over to Hoyt. "We counted three bodies."

"Yeah, he did all the heavy lifting," Hoyt was still regaining his composure. This was only the second gunfight he'd been involved with in his entire career. "There were four perps. One of them made a getaway down Broadway, he disappeared into the crowd towards Times Square."

"They hit Morgan Stanley and made their escape through a fire exit," the cop replied. "It was an inside job, it went real smooth. Whatever busted out their windshield ruined their escape plan. I guess that's when you guys came along."

"Whatever busted their windshield?" Hoyt squinted in disbelief. "There was a woman down there. What happened to her?"

"What woman?"

"Are you kidding me? Don't tell me you didn't get any witnesses."

"It was the damnedest thing. Nobody stepped up. Maybe everybody took off when they heard the gunfire. The people out there had gathered after the shooting started, from all accounts. There wasn't anyone who saw you two take off after the robbers."

"Ask the kid, it all happened out of nowhere," Bob was telling another officer. "We were coming off Columbus Circle when we saw these four guys coming out of the garage carrying black briefcases. They saw something sticking out of the windshield of their illegally parked vehicle and began acting suspiciously. Detective Wexford showed his badge and they took evasive action. I drew my weapon and pursued them, and they began firing at me as they tried to escape. I took one of them out on each level as best I can remember. The first two tried to shoot me, and my return fire took them down from behind. The last one had nowhere to run and tried to take me out in an exchange of gunfire. I was damned lucky, and they weren't."

"Is that how it went down, Detective?"

"Yeah, it was. It happened so fast I was just trying to keep up. I had no idea where my partner was or whether the perps had taken cover. I was also concerned as to whether civilians were being exposed to danger."

"Do you need medical assistance?"

"Well, I could use a beer right about now, but I suppose we'll have to put that off for a few hours."

"Hey, you guys'd better not have towed my Jag!" Bob exclaimed.

"No, the investigation team's just arrived. They won't have a problem with you heading off downtown. Lieutenant Shreve'll be waiting for you."

"What about the girl?" Hoyt insisted.

He rushed towards the ledge overlooking the crime scene and looked down at the black Volvo parked below. He could see the investigators milling around the vehicle with the crushed windshield beneath him.

Only the girl with the long red hair was no longer there.

# Chapter Three

The first of seven DVDs arrived at the offices of Al Jazeera in NYC at 0900 that morning. After a short conference, their executive producers aired the videotaped message on a breaking news segment. Outraged representatives of Homeland Security contacted the studio shortly thereafter, though their anger was quenched by a similar broadcast on CNN and the BBC. Almost immediately afterward, they were contacted by the British, German and French embassies. An emergency meeting was scheduled at the UN after they discussed the DVD they received at their New York headquarters.

"People of New York," a silhouetted figure appeared in a dimly illuminated studio where the Islamic State flag was draped on a back wall. "Once again your Federal Government has failed you and left you unprotected against your enemies. Their half-hearted efforts to prevent the spread of Ebola throughout your communities have failed. Their medical programs to discover a cure for this disease have failed. Most importantly, Homeland Security and law enforcement officials have failed to stop the Islamic State from carrying out its jihad against you."

"I am Apollyon!" the figure thundered. "I am the Angel of Death! I am the demon of ancient prophecy who will pour out the wrath of Allah upon your city, state and nation! There is no way you can escape, no place to where you can turn. Outside of fleeing your homes and leaving New York City forever, I alone am your only hope for survival. Listen to my voice, heed my warning, and obey my command should you wish to avoid the coming tribulation."

"Our scientists have developed a mutant strain of Ebola that is invulnerable to the antidotes concocted by incompetent American scientists. We have not only developed this virus but have also discovered a cure. In exchange for our knowledge, we will accept one hundred million dollars from the American Government. This money is to be delivered according to our instructions. In exchange, we will provide your government the formula to the antidote."

"If this money is not sent to us within the next seventy-two hours, we will release the first of three canisters filled with the Ebola toxin into a heavily populated area of New York City. This will make you realize the gravity of this situation. We will allow you another seventy-two hours before the second plague is unleashed. Should your government continue to defy us, we will deliver the third canister in a manner that will cause the entire planet to stand in shock and awe."

"Do not allow your government to hold your destiny in its hands. Rise up in protest and force them to act in your behalf. People of New York – you are the masters of your fate. Pay our price and spare yourselves the horror of a plague unlike any the world has ever known."

"That jerk needs to fire his speech writer."

Hoyt Wexford and Bob Methot received a hero's welcome when they returned to Police Plaza the next morning. Their fellow officers came over with pats on the backs, high fives, fist bumps and words of encouragement. Hoyt and Bob tried to downplay the accolades, insisting it was just part of the job. Nonetheless, the Organized Crime Unit was in a celebratory mood until Captain Willard and Lieutenant Shreve arrived with a copy of the terrorist's DVD.

"Rest assured that City Hall and the White House are taking this threat very seriously," Willard said after the chuckling subsided. "This thing is a Pandora's Box we need to put the lid back on. We've already gotten messages from Muslim leaders and Arab-American groups across the city assuring us of their support. We've also been updated by research groups who've reported that they've made significant breakthroughs in their Ebola research. The City is standing shoulder-to-shoulder against this lunatic, but we have to move fast. We've got seventy-two hours to shut this guy down. The general consensus is that English is his second language, he's probably a Russian or Eastern European national. We need to work our connections in those ethnic neighborhoods for intel on this guy's network. Bring your snitches in, the dealers, the hookers, everyone on the street who may be able to give us a lead on this nut job."

"You two have an interview with Internal Affairs tomorrow," Shreve came over after the meeting ended. "They got a call from the DoJ[1]. Somebody in Washington thought the incident looked like an execution. They read where Bob was investigated before and decided to look into it."

"Oh, come on, Dwight," Bob exclaimed in disbelief. "You mean you didn't have my back on this?"

"Don't give me that. They had nowhere to run, nowhere to hide, no shots exchanged. I've had your back more times than you can imagine. You know all the heat cops are taking across the country over police brutality. They called your number, Bob. You got to answer."

"Okay, fine. You get me an advocate?"

"Yeah, he'll sit down with you and Hoyt to get your stories straight. In the meantime, I want you two out in Little Odessa. Worst case scenario, if the Feds come down on you two, I want to know you've opened some doors for Don and Jerry."

"Us two?" Hoyt asked. "How does that work?"

"They've got the file on you and the rest of Clyde's team. Even though they know that Alexander Tretiak was crooked, they still got questions about whether you were on the take out there."

"Hey, I already got investigated on that. I came out clean."

"It's DoJ, kid. It's out of our hands."

"What in hell is this about?" Hoyt asked as the partners headed for the parking garage shortly afterward. "What were they looking at you for?"

"I threw some gunslinger off a roof in East Harlem last year. Time before I put one in somebody's head after they tossed their weapon. Heat of the moment, you know how it goes."

"Is that what you told them?"

"Hell no. I'd be selling used cars somewhere if I had."

"Did those Russians toss their weapons in the garage?"

"What difference would it make? We bring them in, their Mob lawyers cut a deal, they're out in five. They still have a hard-on for you, they look you up, one day you're walking your dog and a car hops the curb and runs you over. Bad guys play for keeps these days, kid. So do I."

---

1. Department of Justice

"I can't afford to lose this gig. My fiancé's lying in a coma in Bellevue. The hospital bills got to be siphoning everything she has. I've got to remain solid for her. If we're gonna be a team, we got to watch out for each out, not setting each other up for a fall."

"Don't worry about a thing. If I go down, I'm *not* taking you with me. Besides, I'm not going down. It's gonna take a lot more than some suits from DC to take Bob Methot down. You can take that to the bank, along with all the checks you'll be cashing before you retire from the force some twenty years from now."

Hoyt and Bob parted ways for the rest of the morning. Bob had a meeting with Don and Jerry after their briefing with the Brooklyn Organized Crime Unit later that day. It gave Hoyt enough time to cut loose for his daily visit with Sabrina.

When he walked off the elevator, he caught sight of Shakeera Smith by the nurse's desk and walked straight over to her.

"Hey. I thought you got reassigned."

"No, they asked me to stay on. They liked the way I do her hair. Is there a problem?"

"Not at all. I like the way you do her hair too."

He walked into her room and exchanged frowns with Nurse Ratched, who was opening the blinds and checking Sabrina's bedside equipment.

"Good morning, Detective. I'm sorry to have to tell you you'll have to keep it short and sweet today. She's got some tests scheduled for this afternoon."

"Call me Hoyt, Minnie."

"I prefer to go by Nurse Ratched."

"Well, Minnie, you can call me Hoyt, but think of me as Detective Wexford. We don't want to turn this into the irresistible force versus the immovable object if we don't have to."

"I thought you spoke to Dr. Schumann. I only follow the Doctor's orders. I think he already explained to you the complexity of what we're dealing with here."

"Yeah, yeah. Head injury, nerve damage or psychological trauma, take your pick. Somehow it kinda reminds me of a game of three-card monte."

"What are you suggesting, Detective?"

"I'm suggesting that I may need to find out why this so-called Brooks Foundation considered Schumann – and you – so highly qualified for this job. Now Nurse Smith – Shakeera – I will admit she doesn't disappoint."

"Fifteen minutes, Detective," Minnie said before she left the room.

Hoyt took a seat alongside the bed and was immediately stricken by how beautiful she looked. Shakeera had combed out her titian tresses so they flowed as a scarlet waterfall over her shoulders. Her eyes were lightly touched with mascara and blue shadow, and rouge and lipstick made her appear as a porcelain doll. His eyes filled with tears as he reached out and held her hand.

"My darling," he managed, "you're so beautiful...so beautiful. I can't believe this is happening to us. I know you're a fighter, you're one of the strongest people I've ever met. You've got a wonderful heart that has given so much to so many. I know that heart is going to come through this. My heart, my love, my everything belongs to you. We're going to move on from this. We're going to get married, have children, and share a wonderful life together. Who knows...maybe this...is for the best. We can put this Nightcrawler thing behind us."

He lowered his head and pressed his forehead against her hand.

"You can be so stubborn, Bree. So stubborn."

At once he looked up and saw a twitch beneath her eyelid. He leaped from his chair and rushed to the GCS$^2$ at bedside, trying to decipher its readings. He cursed beneath his breath as it told him nothing.

"That machine ain't no good. Don't tell any more than you can see."

He looked up and saw Shakeera at the doorway.

"I'm glad you stayed on. Me and Minnie don't get on too well."

"Nurse Ratched tough, but she knows her stuff, you can be sure of that."

"Yeah, so does Dr. Schumann and everybody else. It's not doing Bree a whole lot of good."

"You can be sure she getting the best of care. I checks on her all the time. I don't know what it is, but she's gotten real special to me too. I bet she's a wonderful person. I can feel her personality even though I've never heard her voice or looked into her eyes."

"She is wonderful," Hoyt's voice grew husky. "The most wonderful person I've ever known."

Maxim Mironov had been a close friend of Tamerlan Chekhov, but dared not say a word when the order was given to have Tammy killed. He was among the many who were waiting to see what would become of the dreaded Stalingrad

---

2. Glasgow Coma Scale

Sickle Gang. Stanislav Lipki had taken over, and the new Lipki Gang had rallied the troops back into normal operation. Only Max still bore a grudge, and he made a fateful decision in order to avenge his friend's murder.

"What's it going to be then, eh?"

He sat in his bedroom, staring moodily at the smoke-filled bong that permeated the air with the odor of marijuana. He seethed with resentment towards the black-clad figure sitting smugly on the arm of his loveseat. He knew he was being compromised, his very life being placed at risk. Only if he was going to get revenge for Tammy, there would be no better way than this.

"What's it going to be then, eh?"

He considered the fact that Lipki was one of the most vicious leaders in the history of the Russian Mob in Brooklyn. They had beaten Tammy to an inch of his life, and Max and his friends left as the Orthodox priest arrived at his deathbed. He knew the penalty for treason, and they had not even proved that Tammy had betrayed them to this fellow. If they found out that this man was sitting here in this room, he would wish he was dead by the time they were done with him.

"What's it going to be then, eh?"

"What is there, a broken record beneath all that armor?" Max snapped.

"See there, we've got something in common. Most kids these days don't know what a broken record is."

Max flushed at the annoying sound of the figure's electronically-distorted voice. He stared into the dark corner, trying to discern the features of the black mask. It was shapeless, tapered so as to give it no characteristics whatsoever. The poor light reflected off it so that its angles seemed indistinguishable. It looked like a hideous modern art masterpiece.

"You know, I'm having second thoughts about this. My friend Tammy is lying in a box six feet under because of you."

"*Our* friend Tammy nearly helped me break the Russian Mob. You can help me smash the pieces that are left. You know Tammy did it to avenge his brother's death. Together we can avenge Tammy's death. I'm gonna do it with or without you. It'll be a lot quicker with your help."

"I don't like you and I don't trust you. I don't know how Tammy got involved with you in the first place. All I know is, I want to see the people who murdered Tammy rot in hell. If making a deal with the devil – you – will make that happen, then let's do it."

35

"This device is sweep-proof," the Nightcrawler got up and put a tiny chip on the nightstand alongside Max. "They found the one that Tammy planted, but they won't find this one. It deactivates itself when it detects a sweeping device. It goes into sleep mode and doesn't re-activate until the sweep's gone. If the sweep remains in place we install another chip elsewhere."

"Suppose they find it? They'll beat me to death like they did Tammy."

"They *can't* find it. Look, do you think anyone'd work with me if anything happened to you? Besides, if they make you, it justifies what they did to Tammy. I'd never give them that."

"Okay," he exhaled tautly, swiping the chip from the table. "Anywhere in the room works, right?"

"Absolutely anywhere, the more obscure…uh, unfindable…"

"Don't be a smartass, I know what obscure means."

"Let's make this happen," the Nightcrawler rose to leave. "We're gonna avenge Tammy and rid the neighborhood of these bloodsuckers once and for all."

"You don't look so tough," Max challenged as the figure climbed out the window.

"Neither do you," the Nightcrawler replied before vanishing into the darkness.

Max lit a joint and popped a top on a Budweiser, biding time until he heard the knock on his apartment door. He opened it and greeted Carissa, Lori, Chuck and Ron as they entered his tiny living room. They were childhood friends who eventually became his street crew when he began dealing drugs for the Sickle Gang. Although he was continually rebuked by his superiors for confiding in non-Russians, they respected his ability as an earner and allowed the partnership to continue.

"Nice of you to save us some," said Chuck as he took the joint from Max. He was a gay man who was good with a knife.

"There's beer in the fridge," Max replied. "Okay, here's the deal. You drop me off at the club and wait outside. I'll get directions for the pickup and we'll be on our way."

"You want us in behind you after forty-five minutes, right?" Ron asked. He was a tall, slender black man who served in Iraq and Afghanistan.

"Unless I text you first. By that time, it probably means I'm not coming out on my own two feet."

"You take a lot for granted," said Carissa, a beautiful redhead. "Suppose they make us and come down to finish us off?"

"Then I guess I'll meet you guys in hell," Max smirked.

"Not if we see you first," Lori, a lissome blonde, retorted.

"Come on, everyone grab a beer. Let's finish up that joint and get going," Max exhorted them. "The people I'm meeting don't like late arrivals."

Shortly afterward they trotted downstairs and piled into Chuck's panel truck. They cruised to Oceanview Avenue where the Volgograd Social Club was located. Chuck jokingly referred to his truck as the Meat Wagon, and his passengers carefully watched out for used prophylactics and tissue paper before taking a seat. It was only a couple of blocks to the club, and Max clambered out before they headed up the block to wait for him.

"Still riding around with that *pedik*?"

Yuri taunted him as he entered the club.

"He watches my back, I watch his."

"I am very sure he watches your back," Yuri scoffed as the others laughed.

"Funny man. Look, give me my stuff, I'm in a hurry."

"Not so fast," Vitali shot back. "The boss is here. He wants a word."

"Fine," Max shrugged, suddenly cautious of his surroundings. He cursed the Nightcrawler for coming through his window and wondered if he had been seen. Vitali and his brother Timur stood by the door leading to the back room as the Grozny brothers, Pyotr and Nestor, braced him on either side. He felt Yuri coming up behind him and stepped into the room where Stanislav Lipki and two of his enforcers awaited.

"Good evening, Boss," Max said respectfully. "It is good to see you again."

"You don't look so happy," Lipki came around his desk to greet Max. Lipki stood 5'9" and weighed 200 pounds of sinewy muscle. He wore his hair cropped short and favored a well-trimmed beard and mustache. He wore a dark green suit, black shirt and tie, looking very much like a caricature of a Russian mobster replete with diamond pinky ring and thick gold bracelet.

"I would've brought a token if I knew you were here," Max exchanged kisses on each cheek.

"The envelope will do," Lipki smiled. Max drew a packet of $10,000 in hundred-dollar bills from his inside pocket and handed it to Lipki, who slipped it into his suit jacket before returning to his desk.

"Business is good," Max noted.

"It won't be for much longer if that damned Nightcrawler isn't taken out," Lipki replied. "That bank job cost us over two hundred thousand dollars in lost revenue. If it wasn't for Yuri getting away, we would've lost the entire score."

"That was you?" Max turned to Yuri.

"I smell a rat," Yuri growled back. "There was no way that Nightcrawler could've gotten wise to that job."

"So that's what this is?" Max stared at Lipki. "You're accusing me?"

"I agree with Yuri. The job was perfectly planned. We had an insider who gave us details on every inch of the place. They took out the guards and grabbed the money in seconds. Three minutes, in and out. *Kak dva pal'tsa obossat.* A quarter million dollars should have been here on my desk within the half hour. Instead, they find a dead woman in their windshield. Less than five minutes later, three of my men are murdered by the NYPD. The dead woman disappears and the cop gets away clean."

"Maybe the Nightcrawler has someone inside the police department," Max speculated.

"Be quiet when the boss is talking," one of the enforcers growled.

"Let us all speak freely," Lipki held up a hand. "There is no doubt this vigilante is well-connected. Otherwise he would have been caught by now. He was obviously working with the Chechens when we had that feud going last year. Now that we have made the peace, we see that he has turned against the Chechens as well. The Chechens are well aware of the problem and have sent someone to handle it. They want *zassat*, they will get *zassat*. The Evil Angel is here to help solve our problem."

"The Angel of Death," Max said softly. "Is that—the same person who appeared in that video on TV the other day?"

"This is not why we are here. I want you to spread the word to your friends and those in your network. I am offering $250,000 – the amount I lost in that bank robbery – for information leading to the death of the Nightcrawler. For the name of his informer I will pay a half million dollars."

"Why pay twice as much for the informer?"

"I want to make an example, one even greater than that we made of Tamerlan Chekhov. I will start with the traitor, then his family, then his friends. I will avenge our honor tenfold. Ten of his closest family and friends after I kill him. I will leave each of their heads in a trash can on the Coney Island Boardwalk when I am done beating them to death. Do you understand?"

"Yes, my *bugor*," Max nodded. "That is what a traitor deserves."

"You understand. Good. You tell the *goluboy*, the *usbek*, and those two *blyads* of yours. I want their people looking around, asking questions. We also have our resources. Everything will be sent back to our computer banks in Moscow. Our connections in the Federal Security Service are creating a profile of this Nightcrawler. This information will be forwarded to the Evil Angel, who is committed to destroying the Nightcrawler before unleashing the plague in New York City."

"The plague?" Max was dumbfounded. "It will kill everyone, even us."

"We are in Brooklyn, as far from Manhattan as we can get. Think about it, Max. Do you not think that the Americans do not already have an antidote to the Ebola virus? Once they release it, we will replicate it and sell it to the Africans for great profit. There are laboratories throughout Russia and China that are on the verge of discovering the formula. Once we obtain it from the Americans, we will mass-produce it while they are seeking their own approvals from the FDA. The Evil Angel is merely forcing their hand. The $100 million blackmail demand is but a propaganda ploy. It is meant to convince the American people that principle is more important to their government than people's lives."

"Why are you telling me all this?"

"Because I trust you. You are loyal, you have never cheated us of a profit, and you observe the code of silence. The men in this room are disdainful of your friends, but they have all vouched for you. We have been watching you for a while. We think it is time you were given more responsibility."

"Thank you, my *bugor*. I am honored by your trust."

Lipki beckoned his enforcer forth, who handed Max a sizeable plastic baggie.

"There is a pound in there. You should make three times what you normally make. It should be a worthy test of your skill."

"Thank you, my *bugor*," Max glanced at the pound of China White before sticking it into his jacket.

"Tell no one of the Evil Angel. Tell everyone of the bounty on the Nightcrawler and his confederates."

Shortly afterward, Max walked down the street and rejoined his friends in the panel truck.

"How'd it go?" Ron asked.

"Pretty good," Max replied as he climbed into the passenger seat alongside Chuck. "We got a pound of China White."

"A pound," Chuck whistled. "Looks like we're moving up in the world."

"He's testing us. He wants to see what we can do with it," Max said as they began cruising towards Avenue X. "I'll have to weigh it and see if it's a half kilo or a pound. He'll be counting change when we bring the cash in, I can guarantee that."

"You were in there for a while," Chuck said. "What else did he have to say?"

"He wants the Nightcrawler. He's offering a quarter million for the vigilante and a half million for his informants."

"That's because nobody's gonna catch the Crawler," Carissa said, lighting a cigarette as she sat on the floor of the van. "For a half million, people're gonna be turning in everybody. By the end of next week, he's gonna have more names on his desk than the census bureau."

"That's pretty slick," Lori reflected. "I always wondered how those gangsters know so much about people in the neighborhood. They offer these bogus rewards, and they get updates on everybody in Brighton Beach. Makes sense."

"That damn Nightcrawler gotta be working for the government," Ron thanked Carissa for a cigarette. "Anybody else be dead by now. He's been taking down drug dealers, loan sharks, gambling dens, everyone making money for the Mafiya. You remember that thing they had last year about that Russian agent working with the Chechens in that mob war last year. There be people on top pullin' them strings. You know them Chechens ain't got nothin'. That was the Mafiya in Moscow puttin' these bangers in Brighton back in line, you can bet your butts on that."

"That's how it works," Max replied. "You climb too high and someone kicks you off the cliff. I like being down at the bottom where I can enjoy the waterfall."

They stopped for a light and were startled by the appearance of a vehicle that screeched to a halt in front of them. They watched as four men carrying guns surrounded the van and forced Chuck out of the driver's seat.

"Okay, you cooperate and no one gets killed," the leader yanked the passenger door open. "Out of the car, on your hands and knees, now!"

The leader grabbed Max by the collar and forced him to crawl onto the asphalt as he frisked him.

"That's Mob money," Max warned him as the pound of heroin was pulled from his jacket. "You're signing your own death warrant."

"I'll bet they start with you first," the gunman scoffed. He then grabbed Lori by the hair and pulled her from the truck.

"Please don't kill me," she begged, getting up on her knees and wrapping her arms around his waist. "I'll do anything, I swear!"

Lori was an accomplished pickpocket who had spent time in Attica after lifting the wallet of a Federal judge at the Waldorf-Astoria. She had little problem locating the gunman's billfold and pulling it from his pocket before he shoved her to the ground.

"I'd like to take you up on that, but we're kinda in a hurry," the masked man smirked.

"Well, I think you've just run out of time."

Everyone stared at the shadows on the street corner from which a dark figure emerged. The five victims hugged the ground as the gunmen opened fire on the intruder. The attacker responded with what appeared to be electric bolts, exploding into the gunmen and dropping them to the pavement. The Nightcrawler walked over to the leader and confiscated the baggie, then took the pistols from the masked men before they fled into the night.

"Don't take that, they'll kill me for it. Please," Max held his hand out to the vigilante.

"I've got my eye on you," the Nightcrawler tossed the baggie at Max. "I'm watching all of you. Don't let me down."

"Holy crap," Chuck was still shaking. "What was that? What just happened?"

"We gotta talk," Max exhaled tautly. "This isn't the first time."

"You don't mean…" Ron stared at him.

"Look, we got to think this out," Max demanded as they got back in the truck. "He saved us from getting robbed and losing our stash. Plus, he said he's watching us. I know he's watching me. He can burn our butts if we rat him out. We need to work this out so we don't get caught in the middle between him and Lipki."

"All right, let's go to my place and come up with a game plan," Ron decided.

Lori's fingers brushed the wallet in her jacket reassuringly as she climbed into the truck behind the others. Somehow she knew it was going to be her insurance plan as this weird sequence of events unraveled.

\* \* \*

"Mr. Stastny, this is a generous offer and a tremendous opportunity. I don't know how else to say this, but I just don't have the final say in this matter. The CEO of this company has been incapacitated and is unable to approve this project. I would have to get some kind of approval, and it's just not possible under these circumstances."

"Mr. Aeppli, let us be blunt, if you will," Ilya Stastny, the Director of the Russian-Chechen Relations Bureau in Dagestan, sat across from Jon in his office at the Brooks Chemical Company on Staten Island the next morning. "I know all about the BCC's participation in the joint research project with the Russians last year. I know how close you came to developing a cure to the AIDS virus. I also know that the American government left you in the lurch with all that equipment you invested after having pulled the plug on the project. My investors are quite certain that the same equipment can be sued for research-ing the Ebola virus. So certain, in fact, that they are willing to bet ten million dollars that you will be successful."

"Ten million?" Jon swallowed hard.

"Three million up front, which should recoup your investment on equipment and materials. Three million at the mid-point, which will come when you are able to provide scientific proof of a breakthrough in your research and devel-opment. The balance will be payable when you deliver the formula that will be used as a successful remedy to the Ebola virus."

"Mr. Stastny…"

"We have scrutinized the facts and figures presented to us when we made our determination. We know that Miss Brooks set up the Brooks Foundation as an executorship of what is essentially a trust fund. I have no doubt that it is a group of corporate attorneys. We researched the history of the BCC since the passing of Vernon Brooks and the takeover of the company by Miss Brooks. She turned over a sizeable profit over the past year, but it cannot possibly be enough to cover your expenses since the collapse of the AIDS project."

"So you figured you were going to make me an offer I couldn't refuse."

"Not to mention the overabundance of gay males on your staff," Stastny said kindly. "I have no doubt that they were greatly disappointed in the negative outcome. We must also consider the enormous toll the Ebola outbreak is having on AIDS victims, what with their decreased ability to resist infection. If they were to find out that the BCC turned down yet a second opportunity to save the victims of these diseases in the gay community…"

"Are you trying to blackmail me, Mr. Stastny?"

"Blackmail is a rather strong word, Mr. Aeppli. Blackmailers extort people for money or services in exchange for their silence. I am a businessman trying to negotiate a deal which will greatly profit both of us. You will be able to take your company to the next level with ten million dollars, not to mention the historic achievement with which you would be accredited. My backers will be able to reproduce the serum and save lives around the world."

"At a hefty profit, I'm sure."

"Well, let us consider the fact that Dagestan is no longer a communist country."

They managed to share a chuckle.

"Look, I have people I'm responsible to. I need to discuss this with them before I can make a decision. There's also all the red tape we had to deal with back before we took on the AIDS project. I'm not sure we have the resources we had when Sabrina was running things."

"You talk to your people, and I'll deal with mine," Stastny was reassuring. "I am quite certain that both your government and the Russians will be more than glad to step aside and let us run with the ball, as you might say. My people will deal with the red tape. We will draw up the necessary documents and forward them for the approval of your Brooks Foundation. Just think of what could happen if an antidote was not developed? What with the recent threats made by that terrorist, that madman who appeared on TV the other day."

"Apollyon," Jon shook his head. "First the Octagon, then Tryzub, now this. Where do these psychopaths come from? What is this world coming to? Aren't things bad enough without these maniacs trying to profit from it?"

"There are people who are working to change things for the better. People like you and me. People like the Nightcrawler."

"Yeah, the Nightcrawler," Jon involuntarily flinched as if Stastny had touched a raw nerve. "If there really is a Nightcrawler. Who knows if there's a bunch of vigilantes out there running around in disguise taking the law in their own hands? Who knows where that's going? Suppose all those teenage mutant ninja turtles start robbing banks next? You can bet your bottom dollar that everybody's going to pin in on the Nightcrawler – or everyone they suspect of being the Nightcrawler."

"It sounds like you've put a lot of thought into it."

"Well, it's hard not to think about it. It's all over the media these days. If you were a New Yorker, you'd understand why people might feel somewhat indebted to him. He put the Octagon and Tryzub out of commission. It's hard to watch him take a bum rap for stuff he didn't do. That's the way things are these days. It's all media spin. Maybe he'll have enough sense to quit while he's ahead – if he hasn't quit already."

"Yes, and let people like you and I do what we can to save the world. I'm sure Miss Brooks would agree."

"Yeah," Jon said quietly. "I'm sure Sabrina would agree."

# Chapter Four

Sabrina dreamt of a time when she and her father woke up early one morning and took a drive out to Long Island Sound to go fishing. It was a very special time for her as she and her Dad got to spend the whole day alone together. She noticed that she was probably the only ten-year-old girl out there. Most of the other people were groups of men or fathers with their sons. She was very proud that she was able to go out and share time the way boys usually did with their Dads.

"Honey, can you bring me that container of worms from the cooler?" Vernon asked her as he began sorting out their fishing gear along the shoreline. He picked a spot by the tree where the grassy knoll gave way to a gentle slope leading to the water. There were some boulders nearby where they could sit and lower their lines without scaring off the fish if they moved about. Sabrina felt as if they had found their own special place in the whole world.

"Ewww!" she winced as she peeked inside the container. "Where'd you get those things?"

"They're nightcrawlers," he chuckled. "The fellow at the bait shop says he gets them special from Canada."

"Here," she handed him the container.

"Thanks."

"Say, Daddy," she said as she watched him put one of the worms on a hook. "Wouldn't it be something if you could turn real ugly like a nightcrawler whenever you wanted? You could scare anybody anytime anywhere. Do you think maybe sometimes ugly people are kinda lucky?"

"Now, come here," he got serious.

"Oh boy," she rolled her eyes, knowing a father-daughter chat was coming.

"I'm not mad," he explained, petting her hair. "I just want you to think about that. Ugly people are the way they are just like everybody else. They can't help the way God made them. You know He looks at us the way we are on the inside, and that's the way we have to look at them. It's just like crippled people, or sick people, or all the other people who aren't as fortunate as you are. You always have to look at people the way God looks at them."

"I'm sorry, Daddy. I didn't mean anything."

"I know you didn't," he hugged her before kissing her head and ruffling her hair. "I just want you to remember that."

"Daddy?" she asked as she peeked into the canister again. "Does that mean that nightcrawlers are cute in their own way?"

"Well, I'm not sure that I'd agree with that," he wrinkled his nose.

"Me neither!" she slapped the top back on the canister. "Ewww!"

Hoyt Wexford thought he saw movement beneath her eyelids, but it was so fleeting that he could not be certain. He held her hand for a second, and in leaning over he noticed a book in the back of her nightstand that had not been there before. He pulled it out and inspected it thoroughly before Nurse Ratched entered the room.

"Say, Nurse, what's this?"

"Looks like a book to me."

"Very funny. It's a book on curare."

"I thought it might be interesting," Ratched grew defensive for the first time Hoyt could remember. "I believe Dr. Schumann feels that no stone should be left unturned."

"Did he mention that to you? Did he say anything about her possibly being poisoned?"

"Well, let's say that things are pretty strange outside that door. You've got all these different Government people lurking around out there, along with all those foreigners and the like. Sometimes I feel like I stepped into the middle of a movie. I pride myself on keeping on top of current events, Detective. I know Ms. Brooks had a contract with a Russian enterprise before she had her accident. I have to question what they want here while she's in recovery."

"Talk about a conspiracy theory," Hoyt sniggered. "Maybe they don't want the truth to come out about why the Government pulled the plug on the AIDS project."

"You tell me," Ratched gave him a look before she left the room with an armful of used linen. "You're the detective."

At once the implications of Ratched's words swept over him like a sheet of hot water. He strode out into the corridor and stared about, his blood beginning to boil as he caught sight of Kelly Stone near the visitors' area.

"Stone," Hoyt walked up to him. "Didn't I make it clear that you people aren't welcome here?"

"Well, this may or may not concern you," Kelly replied. "I was actually hoping to catch Rita here. She said she was coming up to visit Sabrina today."

"You've gotta be kidding me. Rita's a churchgoer. You think she's gonna become another notch on your bedpost?"

"Whoa, let's back it up a second. Who made you the social director around here? I'm not sure who Rita makes friends with is any of your business. What I am sure of is that you'd better think twice before you start passing judgment on me or meddling in my business."

"It just so happens that Rita's one of Bree's best friends. You can be damned sure that I'm not gonna let some slickster from Washington take advantage of her."

"Let me tell you something, buddy, you're really pressing your luck here."

"Well, hello there, guys."

They were both caught unawares at the sight of Rita Hunt approaching them. She was breathtaking in her form-fitting midnight blue dress suit and white silk stockings. She carried a bouquet of flowers to place at Sabrina's bedside. They greeted her warmly as she failed to notice the withering looks exchanged between them.

"Why, hello, Hoyt!" she came over and exchanged hugs with him and Kelly. "How lucky can I be to catch you both here at the same time. I got a wonderful invitation from Pastor Mitchell and I'll be able to include both of you."

"Uh, I thought I was gonna be taking you to lunch," Kelly was disappointed.

"Nope, I'm taking you," she said merrily. "The Pastor got an invitation from the United Federation of Christian Churches in Dagestan the other day. They sent him VIP coupons for four at the Russian Tea Room. It's being sponsored by the Dagestan Embassy. I looked up their website on the Internet, it looks swell!"

"When does it start?" Kelly asked.

"If we leave now we'll be right on time."

They caught a cab to the luxurious restaurant on West 57$^{th}$ Street, Rita sitting up front and chatting gaily with their Jamaican driver. There was a notable distance between Hoyt and Kelly in the back seat. They considered each other unwelcome but did not want to ruin this event for Rita. Both of them perceived that she was deeply moved at the sight of Sabrina in her affliction but was doing her best to hide it from them. They decided they would make the best of the situation and make it as pleasant for her as possible.

Regardless of their frame of mind, they could not help but be glad for her as they were escorted by the maître d' to the Hearth Room. It was an exquisite setting with domed ceilings and lamps subtly illuminating the paneled walls and wonderfully-set tables positioned before the fabled fireplaces. Rita was as a young girl in a china shop, marveling at the exquisite furnishings and touching their sleeves when she noticed something of particular charm.

"Rita! I'm so glad you made it!"

Pastor Matt Mitchell exchanged hugs with Rita as the two law enforcement officers sized up the figure looming behind him. The man stood six-foot-six at 280 pounds, his close-cropped hair and beard reminding them of a youngish Gary Busey without the keyboard teeth. He dwarfed the two men flanking him, both six-footers as big as Hoyt and Kelly.

"Everybody, this is Dzhokhar Zhivago, the Assistant Secretary to the Foreign Minister of Dagestan," the Pastor smiled as the giant stepped forth. He was re-splendent in a $5,000 charcoal suit, white shite and black tie. Both men thought he made a show of kissing Rita's hand before catching theirs in a vise-like grip.

"I'm sorry, was that Joker?" Hoyt could not help himself.

"It's pronounced Zho-kar, my friend," they perceived a glint in his eye.

"You don't have to be a dick," Kelly whispered as they were escorted to their table.

"Neither does he," Hoyt hissed quietly.

They were delighted by the caviar tasting option as appetizers before the Boeuf a la Stroganoff was served. Hoyt and Kelly found it harder to mind their tongues as they were treated to the exquisite vodka menu, the Pastor and Rita settling for iced tea.

"In case you haven't seen *Titanic*, you start the silverware at the end and work your way in," Hoyt told Kelly as the waiters took the caviar plates away.

"Yeah, well, that cloth near your plate has a special purpose too," Kelly retorted.

"Pardon?" the Pastor asked amicably, within earshot of their ribbing.

"Just kidding," they chorused.

"So, my dear, I understand you were a friend of Dariya Romanova," Zhivago sat at the head of the table with Rita to his right alongside the Pastor.

"Oh, yes," Rita tried her best to remain jovial though the memory of Dariya's funeral was intensely painful. Sabrina had just been admitted to the hospital and did not attend. "She and Bree and I were very close."

"I myself was a very close friend of the Romanova family," he revealed. "They were greatly bereaved by news of her passing and reached out to me for whatever I could find out about her. Of course, they knew she was a prominent researcher in Moscow. It was the intimate details they were most interested in. What she liked to do, what it was like for her in New York, who her friends were."

"There's just so much to tell. She was such a complex person. You couldn't define her by her career or her background. She was so much like Bree in the way she related to people. There wasn't anything you couldn't talk to her about. She was so wonderful. I—it's hard to realize that I've lost two of my closest friends so suddenly. Just like that"

"I understand, my dear. Let us not discuss it further. Perhaps I can call you later in the week when you've had time to think about it. Let us exchange business cards and we can meet at a more convenient time."

"That would be just fine."

Kelly glanced at Hoyt with a look of disbelief, realizing how he had been line-jumped.

"I'm with you, dude. In my book, you're the lesser of two evils."

"Pardon?" the Pastor put his finger to his ear. "It's kinda noisy in here."

\* \* \*

"It was the worst night of my life," Hoyt recalled. "I'd just survived that shootout where my entire team got killed. Lieutenant Shreve told me to chill out, take things easy, but there was too much going on. I had my radio on and heard there had been an incident at the BCC. I drove over there just as they were loading Dariya's body into the ambulance. They said she'd been thrown through the second floor window and broke her neck. It wasn't but a couple of hours later that we got the report that Bree had survived an explosion in Lower Manhattan that killed four Boko Haram terrorists."

Hoyt and Kelly decided to bury the hatchet and picked up a pint of Courvoisier before heading down to the Brooklyn Bridge. They had the taxi drop them off near the River Café and strolled out by the pier together to make the peace.

"I read the report a hundred times," Kelly took a swig of cognac before handing the bottle to Hoyt. "Those murderous bastards, how could have they done that? Two beautiful women like that. You talk about remorseless killers. What the hell made them throw her out that window?"

"They were obviously trying to leverage Bree. Those were two headstrong women. They couldn't get what they wanted so they killed Dariya. Bree still wouldn't give them what they wanted so they brought her to that warehouse. She outsmarted them somehow, but it wasn't enough."

"I just don't get the part why she dressed up like the Nightcrawler," Kelly said quietly. "Nobody can. Especially when her boyfriend was an NYPD detective. You'd think she could've trapped those bastards without putting her life on the line."

"If she never wakes up, I'll go to my grave asking why," Hoyt exhaled, staring across the East River at the Lower Manhattan skyline. "Two innocent women against a gang of murderers."

"Do you think she had a connection? With the Nightcrawler?"

"Come on, dude. Are you frickin' kidding me?" Hoyt stared at him.

"Hey, chill out," Kelly held out his hand. "We're cool. My people have already stood down. I don't know if you realize we've spotted some persons of interest around Bellevue."

"What?"

"Damn, Hoyt, do you think we were there waiting to grill Sabrina? We got word through the grapevine about Russian nationals with prison records going in and out of the hospital for no apparent reason. We hauled a couple of them in but they wouldn't give us jack. We're grasping at straws here. We think there might be a link between Boko Haram and the Muslim extremists in Dagestan, but who can prove anything these days? This is Osama Bin Laden's wet dream. They're all in bed together one minute and burning each other down the next. Nobody's trying to crucify your fiancé, Hoyt. We're just trying to find out who she talked to last."

"All right," Hoyt conceded. "You and I understand each other. Just give us some space. You have resources, you can help me out. Keep your people off her floor at the hospital and I'll give you what I get in Brighton. Maybe if we pool our resources we can take these guys down."

"Once we figure out who it is we're taking down," Kelly shook his head.

"Man, have you lost your mind! You cut a deal with the Nightcrawler? We're dead, man! We're all dead!"

"Look, why don't you just chill out! He saved our asses, don't forget! What do you think would've happened if we'd have gotten jacked for a pound of China White just a couple of blocks from Lipki's clubhouse?"

Max and his friends drove to Ron's house to get their heads together after the incident near Avenue X that fateful night. After they smoked a joint, Max confessed his association with the Nightcrawler that left them all astounded.

"The way I see it, we either leave town or we're all dead," Carissa shook her head. "Even if we ratted you out to Lipki, he'd kill us because he hates us."

"What are you saying, you'd rat me out?" Max leaped from his seat.

"I'm just saying, that's not even an option. Just chill out, dude, we're *all* screwed, thanks to you."

"All right, let's just put everything in perspective," Chuck insisted. "If the Nightcrawler's got Max's back – our back – it's a plus. He's pinned the entire Mafiya's ears back. Why do you think they've got that lopsided reward out? He's all over the place, he's cost them thousands of dollars. How else could've he stopped those guys from ripping us off? Maybe he's got cameras hidden all over Brighton. Maybe it's like the tabloids say, maybe he's getting paid off by the cops."

"Maybe my ass," Lori seemed panicky. "That half million reward's for real. My mother would turn me in for a half million dollars."

"She would not," Chuck waved her off.

"Well, my aunt would, that bitch."

"We need to put things in perspective," Ron decided. He was in his forties and considered the voice of reason. "Maybe we can just chill out, lay low and not move anything until things settle down. We'll see how things go with the Nightcrawler, maybe they'll kill the bastard by then."

"Are you nuts?" Max sat back down after putting a Lady Gaga CD on Ron's console. "Lipki just gave us a pound to move. He upped us from a third of a ki. You think he's expecting us to sit on it? He'll send those dickheads from the club to find out what's up. I told you from the get, these people don't jack around. You saw what they did to Tammy."

"There," Lori was emphatic. "There you go. I went to school with Tammy. They had a closed coffin at his funeral."

"Look, that's not what I meant," Max shot back. "I'm not saying that's what they'll do to us, but that's what they *could* do to us. We got to move on like this never happened. None of it, not the jacking, not the Nightcrawler, none of it. Business as usual. Look, those guys who tried to jack us weren't amateurs. They'll try it again, and Lipki'll find out. This'll sail right past us if we maintain our cool. Just make the usual sales but don't look for new connections. Lay low, chill out, let the business come to us until things cool down."

He broke the pound bag into five portions of five ounces each, keeping the extra ounce himself. They would have to cut it down to keep their buyers from overdosing. After paying off their dealers, they could expect to earn five hundred dollars apiece for a couple of days' work.

"People say this is the best stuff out there," Ron stuffed his baggie in his pocket. "I'm expecting it to move real quick."

"Don't forget what I said," Max reminded them before they departed for the evening. "Tell your dealers, no new business. If any new faces show up, make them get three references before they make the sale. This way if anyone gets busted, I've got some names to give to Lipki."

"Three references," Chuck sighed. "Whatever happened to the good old days?"

"They're with the old dealers doing time in Attica," Max growled.

Philemon Rubidium watched with trepidation as the latest shipment of cardboard boxes was being unloaded at the 137th Street Mosque. Since the murder of the elders by Kamala Brown, the mosque had been taken over by Donna Summer and cell leaders of Boko Haram. Although the traditional signs and banners of Islam remained in place on the main floor, the basement was festooned with Islamic State flags and those of Boko Haram. The cardboard boxes were torn away so that what appeared to be crates of guns and ammo were stacked against the walls.

"Remember, nigger," the Africans would taunt him whenever he appeared to be having second thoughts. "If you backslide in your faith we will kill everyone in your family. We will set fire to the entire block where you live."

His greatest fears were being realized as Donna Summer had rented the Apollo Theatre for an Islamic rally. It would lend unprecedented prestige to the mosque on a level the Black Muslims had not seen since Malcolm X's prayer meetings of the Sixties. Only Donna's speeches had grown increasingly radicalized as she openly called for the rise of the black race against their white slavemasters. She exhorted Black Muslims to join in global jihad to establish the Caliphate as the ruling power throughout the planet.

"Sister Donna," Philemon pleaded as she sat in his office, inspecting documents and memos as plans for the revival were being finalized. "I am being besieged by the families of the missing elders who are demanding word from their relatives. No one is buying our story that the elders packed up and left for Nigeria to join the Islamic State. They are threatening to report this to the FBI."

"You will give the names of the murmurers to Brother Kamala, and he will deal with them accordingly," Donna slammed her fist on his desk. "I have more important things to worry about than covering up the murders of eleven dead backsliders!"

"Sister Donna," he pleaded. "Let me go back and reason with them. There has been enough bloodshed."

"Very well. Is there anything else?"

"Well, yes," Philemon hesitated. He had been forced to take his own paperwork to the smaller receptionist's desk outside his office. "I will have to check my notes, but... it seems like we are getting a lot of pushback from the municipalities against your rally. Both the Mayor and even the Governor has expressed doubts about the wisdom of holding such an event in the midst of the Ebola epidemic. We have gotten numerous calls from members of Congress as well. They feel we are disregarding the public health and safety of our people for gain of publicity and recognition."

"Fool!" she blazed, slapping her coffee cup off the desk so that it shattered against the wall. "Do you not see that it is a feeble attempt by the white man to keep us from reaching our goal? What happened to your faith, my big-head brother? Is your head that much bigger than your heart? Do you not believe that Allah can protect his followers from the plague, just as Moses protected our people from the plagues of Egypt?"

"No, no," Philemon cowered as he jumped up to retrieve the cup and wipe coffee off the wall with his handkerchief. "It is just that the black community is being hit harder by Ebola than the whites and the Hispanics. Forty percent of our people have been afflicted by the virus. The hospitals in our communities are being overwhelmed by patients seeking treatment. If just one person brings the virus to our rally, the ripple effect could be disastrous."

"Coward!" she came around the desk, her six foot frame towering over the kneeling Philemon in her high heels. "You sound like the white propaganda broadcasters! Who creates these statistics, white men or blacks? Infidels or Muslims? Consider the source and face your fears accordingly. Fear not the white man who enslaves the body, but Allah who owns your very soul!"

"I believe, Sister! I believe!" he cringed, adjusting his glasses before they fell from his face.

"Good," she reached down and patted his head. "Now go about your tasks. Get me the names of any who have spoken of the FBI. I want to make sure they are not as well protected by Allah as the brothers and sisters who will join us at the rally next week."

Lieutenant Leroy Chandler was known as Angel Eyes when he first started as a beat cop in the NYPD. Though he seemed affable at first glance, those who knew him said his pale blue lizard eyes betrayed his cold-blooded Machiavellian instincts. Hoyt Wexford had crossed swords with him when Clyde Giroux and Alexander Tretiak were making inroads into his territory. Now Hoyt was back with a different team, but it made Chan no less wary.

"The problem is that the movers and shakers at Police Plaza don't understand the Russian Mob," the grey-haired black man insisted as he stared across his desk at Hoyt. They sat in his office that afternoon at the 60$^{th}$ Precinct on West 8$^{th}$ Street off Surf Avenue. "They think the Russian Mafiya controls the Chechen Mob, but it's the other way around. People think the Tryzub came over here to steal the apple cart. What they did was shake the rotten apples down from the apple tree. They own the apple cart. The Russian Mob's just selling apples for them."

"What about the fact that the Chechens, particularly from Dagestan, are predominantly Muslim? There's no denying that. I went head–to-head with those guys. They knocked off my whole team and nearly put me six feet under."

"The Chechens in Dagestan are working for Russian Jewish mobsters who control the Mafiya in Moscow. They are being developed as an elite killing machine, much like the American Mafia had their Murder Incorporated in the Fifties. The entire Russian Mob fears the Chechens, and the top Mafiya leaders rely on them as their Praetorian Guard. Tryzub was sent here to restore order within the ranks and eliminate the bosses who had grown fat and greedy. Once they staged their *coup d'etat*, they allowed the next generation of leaders to step up and assume command with a new understanding of the Chechen Mob."

"So what advice can you give me?" Hoyt insisted. "I've got this Nightcrawler Squad that's assigned to track down someone who lots of people – including me – don't think is the original item. Our problem is that this fellow is in the midst of a war against the Chechens. He may not live long enough for us to take him into custody."

"Now, you're seriously telling me you're here to take down the Nightcrawler. Dwight Shreve didn't send you here to get in my good graces so you could pick up where you left off."

"I already told you that I was the low man on that totem pole. Clyde Giroux was trying to break down the Russians the only way he knew how, by bleeding them dry. I still think Alex Tretiak was a Russian spy sent by the Federal Security Service to direct that coup you talked about. They only denounced him after I killed him in self-defense during that ambush."

"I think one day you and I have to break open a bottle of Scotch and discuss it sometime."

"Not happening. Commissioner Jordan had it all declared top-secret. I'd lose my job and face criminal charges if they found out I was yakking about it."

"Be that as it may," Chan weaved his fingers together. "So you think you can keep a secret. Suppose I told you I had my own elite team who's been putting a bigger dent in the Chechens' operation than the Nightcrawler?"

"That would certainly be a major piece of information."

"What would you give me in return?"

"Full cooperation. You know what kind of pull Shreve has at the Plaza. If I was working with your guys, they would have access to resources that might not be available here in Brooklyn."

"Like what?"

"Okay, let's bargain. I've got a major player with Homeland Security who's crossed paths with me at Bellevue following my fiancée's accident. He's grasping for straws trying to connect the dots between the Islamic State, the Chechens and Boko Haram. If your team and mine could get him some intel, he might just be able to give us enough to capsize this new Mafiya regime."

"Yeah," Chan sat cross-legged in his swivel chair, raising a finger in the air. "The NYPD couldn't get past first base against the Gambino Family in the 90s until the Feds stepped in. If your guy can help us set up a RICO indictment, maybe we wouldn't get the glory but we'd certainly gain the victory."

"What does your elite team got going right now?"

"Right now they've been playing a game of shadows with Stanislav Lipki. He's starting to look like he may end up as the acting boss here in Brooklyn until the Russians anoint the next kingpin. Lipki's highly cautious and he's got plenty of combat experience. Especially after ending up as the last man standing after the coup. The rank and file refer to him as the *Avtorityet*, which is the official title for a Russian capo. He's got five capable men as lieutenants who are loyal unto death. We've been harassing and interdicting their sergeants, but so far it's been all probing maneuvers. We're trying to identify their hub resources so we can put a serious plan together."

"What's he got going for himself besides drugs?"

"Plenty. There's prostitution, pornography, loan sharking, stock market scams and insurance fraud, not to mention the legitimate industries they've bought into. My biggest concern is as to whether he has any connections with that madman Apollyon. The Ebola epidemic is costing us millions of dollars a day here in Brooklyn. If the contagion begins to spike, it could result in cut-backs that could derail my project."

"Yeah, money talks and BS walks," Hoyt exhaled. "Well, look, if you let me work with your guys, we can probably keep the spigot open. I'm pretty sure I can get Shreve to request emergency funds for the special project, and if that runs out we can hit up my HS guy."

"So how does this work? We just go on spit and a handshake?"

"Unless you have any forms I can sign in blood, I guess that's how it'll go."

"All right. I'll send you an e-mail, you and one of your guys go undercover to meet two of my men. See if you hit it off."

"I don't follow. Isn't your word good enough?"

"Not in this case. My guys are deep undercover and their lives are on the line. If they don't think they can work with you, I'm not pushing them into anything, special funding or not."

"Wow, I'm impressed," Hoyt grinned. "These must be some really special guys."

"I'll let you judge for yourself."

Hoyt drove back to Flatbush and found a Subway restaurant where he could have lunch and access the Internet on WiFi. He bagged half his six-footer and was on his third cup of coffee when he finally got an e-mail from Chan. At that, he called Bob Methot on his cell phone.

"Yeah."

"We got a meet at O'Keefe's at Borough Hall with Chan's guys."

"That'll work. I need to stop by OTB."

"Are you kidding? We need to be there at four sharp."

"You keep my seat warm."

"Bob, don't screw around. These guys are heavy hitters."

"What are we, chopped liver? They'll keep."

The line went dead.

Hoyt drove down to the Brooklyn Bridge and parked near the Watchtower complex, walking up to Court and Montague Streets. He knew what parking was like at Borough Hall at rush hour and would not ever consider it. The ten-minute walk helped him get his head together, and he was all business as he weaved his way through lawyers, cops and college kids to the end of the long bar at the hallowed pub. He ordered a pitcher and set two mugs in front of two stools as he waited impatiently for Methot.

"Hey."

"Hey yourself. You're late, dude."

"What am I, wearing a cowboy hat and jeans?"

"They said four on the dot."

"Yeah, well, where the hell are they?"

"Excuse me, gentlemen," the buxom blonde barmaid came over, pouring shots of Remy Martin in front of them. "These are on your friends."

She nodded towards two scruffy-looking bearded men in ski caps and Army jackets engaged in conversation over a pitcher in the last booth near the jukebox. Hoyt and Bob picked up their drinks and walked over.

"Mind if we join you?"

"Who the hell are you?"

"NYPD," Bob pulled his suit jacket open to show his gun and badge.

"Yeah, you look the part," the men sidled over.

"So you guys're working Brighton."

"That's what we hear."

"Come across any Nightcrawlers lately?"

"Maybe. Maybe not," the broad-shouldered black-haired man growled. Up close the detectives could see their mustaches and goatees were fake.

"We need to bring him in for debriefing. We'll do whatever it takes. If you can help us, we'll do whatever we need to in helping your job get done."

"Who says we need help?"

"Your boss. This Ebola epidemic's draining your cash reserves. If that sicko Apollyon makes good on his threat, it could close half the city down. They'll pull the plug on you guys."

"Who says we won't keep it going on our spare time?"

"Look," Hoyt leaned forward. "We got Federal connections. We can bring state-of-the-art high-tech gear to the table. You can get a hell of a lot more done than you can doing the weekend warrior thing."

"We're already running them to the ground. They're sick and they're tired."

"Let's cut the crap. I'm Bob Methot."

"We know who you are. He's Hoyt Wexford. You're teamed with Loverdi and Conroy. The guys we're up against have been trained by ex-Spetsnaz commandos in Dagestan. They have their own state-of-art gear. You can't carry what it takes to stand up to these guys. It's all hit and run. One mistake and you're wasted."

"The Nightcrawler's been doing okay."

"The Nightcrawler hasn't gone up against these guys. When he does, it may be the end of the line for him. We're trying to get to them before they get to the vigilante."

"That's kinda ironic," Hoyt felt his gut involuntarily tightening. "The Nightcrawler has literally become live bait."

"You could say that," the curly-haired tall man nodded.

"So deal us in," Bob said.

"We'll think it over. You'll get an e-mail from Chan."

The four cops rose from the table before the two scruffy men headed through the crowd out the door. Hoyt and Bob followed them outside and watched as a compact black car pulled up in front of them at the curb. The men got in the back seats before the vehicle zipped off into traffic.

"Think these guys can back themselves up?"

"I guess we're gonna find out," Hoyt replied.

"You parked nearby?"

"Under the Bridge."

"C'mon, I'll give you a ride."

Hoyt walked down Montague Street with Bob, realizing that he was about to undertake one of the most dangerous missions of his career.

He only hoped he was equal to the task.

# Chapter Five

The next morning just before noon, a crowd was gathering in front of the Freedom Tower at One World Trade Center. It started as an Internet rumor that Donna Summer planned an impromptu rally in front of the renowned building to unite blacks and Muslims against police brutality. It attracted civil rights activists and social agitators across the city, and soon thousands of people gathered to participate in the event. Word soon reached Police Plaza, where Captain Willard ordered riot police in full gear to keep control over the demonstration. Shortly thereafter there were outbursts that drew the media. As it turned out, it was a cleverly staged hoax by the Black Muslims that Donna Summer had no intention of attending.

The attention of New Yorkers throughout Lower Manhattan was so riveted on the transpiring events that no one even noticed the gasoline truck speeding towards the Wall Street area. No one could have guessed that the tank had been filled with sewage water contaminated by the Chechens' Ebola formula. Nor would they have imagined that the bed of the truck had been filled with forty sticks of dynamite.

"This is a great blow we will strike in the name of Allah," the driver gloated as they drove through a red light, causing another vehicle to swerve violently in avoiding a collision. "The infidels will choke on this stew you have prepared, my brother."

"According to social media, there are over ten thousand people gathering near the target area," the giant sitting alongside him studied his Blackberry. "Once the bomb is detonated, those who are not killed will be evacuated and will spread the contaminant. The hospitals will become the new sources of the plague, and all who are taken there will surely die."

The black man chortled at the thought and sped on until, at once, he spotted a form lying in the middle of the street.

"What is that?" he stared at the figure. "What the hell? It's a stiff!"

The giant looked through the windshield at the body of a redheaded woman curled in a fetal position just yards ahead of them. The driver veered to his left to avoid splattering the body. As a result, he ran right over an uncovered manhole which had no emergency signs around it. The front tires of the massive truck dropped into the hole, breaking the axle and causing the truck to crash onto its bumper in the middle of the street.

"Boy, you guys can't drive worth a darn, huh?"

The passenger door of the truck was forced open so that the giant was able to climb free. He stood nearly seven feet tall, clad in a metallic blue armored suit with a helmet that shielded his features. He spotted the shape standing defiantly before him and slowly began stalking his prey.

"They're making them big in Russia these days. I didn't think you could stack garbage that high."

"I am Apollyon. You will die with my name on your lips."

With that, Apollyon tackled the Nightcrawler, driving the vigilante across the street into a parked car. The giant pressed a lever on his glove, causing a steel hook to dart from a metal bar on his right forearm. He drove the hook with all his might at his opponent's head, who managed to dodge at the last second. The hook punctured the hood of the car, allowing the Nightcrawler to pull free as the giant yanked his weapon loose.

"So you wanna play rough, eh?" said the black-clad figure, driving a steel-toed boot deep into the back of the giant's knee before hammering him across the jaw with a titanium-studded right fist. Apollyon reeled backward, waiting for the Nightcrawler to close in before lunging with a crushing right that sent the vigilante flying over the hood of the parked car.

"Ow!" the Nightcrawler said after bouncing off a parking meter onto the sidewalk. "I'll get you for that."

"You little bastard, I'll beat you to death!"

Apollyon turned sideways to make his way between the parked cars before him just as the Nightcrawler drew a weapon and fired. A stream of white powder hit him directly in the mask, immediately blinding him and cutting off his oxygen.

"*Aack...*" he gurgled as mucus filled his eyes and throat.

"Now let's see how big and tough you are," the Nightcrawler holstered the weapon.

At once, a black sedan screeched to a halt behind Apollyon. A black man wearing a kerchief over his face fired a spray of bullets at the Nightcrawler, causing the dark figure to duck for cover. Another man grabbed Apollyon's arm and steered him into the vehicle. The car streaked away, barely avoiding the redheaded figure lying in the road ahead.

"Okay, so apparently they're playing hardball," Captain Willard opened the emergency meeting at Police Plaza a couple of hours later. "Our guys discovered the truck loaded with liquid waste treated with what is suspected to be an Ebola-based contaminant. That psychopath Apollyon was obviously intent on making good on his threat. We have videos flooding the Internet posted by onlookers who saw the altercation between Apollyon and the Nightcrawler."

"So if the Nightcrawler is seven foot tall, this guy must go about ten feet," a cop grunted.

"We'll be studying this train wreck for months," Lieutenant Shreve replied. "Even though the matter at hand is Apollyon, we finally have some actual footage of the Crawler. We're figuring our guy's probably about five-ten, one hundred eighty tops. Apollyon's got to be almost seven feet, at least three hundred. In other words, Apollyon's as big as some people thought the Crawler was."

"What about Deadwoman? Do they figure she's somewhere in between?"

There was a significant amount of video footage depicting the figure of the woman lying in the middle of Broadway. Only a couple of people caught sight of the Nightcrawler gathering up the woman in a fireman's carry and trotting down a side street to escape. News about the Nightcrawler's new partner Deadwoman went viral, getting almost as much attention as the fight between Apollyon and the vigilante.

"Look, the Lieutenant already made it clear that this meeting isn't about the Nightcrawler, much less this so-called Deadwoman," Willard was emphatic. "What I will say is that it supports Wexford and Methot's statement about the armed robbery near Columbus Circle a few days ago."

"Maybe the Deadwoman's a stunt double from Hollywood or something," a cop mused.

"Enough of Nightcrawler and Deadwoman," Shreve insisted. "Our focus is on that madman who nearly created a new epidemic a couple of hours ago.

We have to find this guy at all costs. Leave no stone unturned, call in all your markers. Obviously this psycho's working with black gang members who may or may not be linked to that Boko Haram group uptown. We can see that they're trying to play the race card, but that's not gonna work for them. I don't care if they're white, black, yellow or green. If you come across anyone who even jokes about setting off another dirty bomb, they go up against the wall for probable cause. I know we've been taking a lot of heat for stop and frisk tactics lately, but there's no choice at all here. We have to shut this guy down before he shuts this city down."

"So how's this going to affect our objectives?" Bob put on his shades as he and Hoyt headed to the garage after the meeting. "Are we gonna start keying in on Deadwoman?"

"The Deadwoman's just a decoy," Hoyt replied. "She went through that windshield to prevent the bank robbers from escaping last week. She laid down in the road to block that gasoline truck today. I just can't figure how the Nightcrawler is letting someone take those kind of risks, especially a woman. That's not the way he normally operates."

"Maybe he's finally decided to let someone else share the risk. Diving off the Statue of Liberty, then a Goodyear blimp, duking it out with the Reaper, then Apollyon...I'd hate to be this guy's insurance broker."

"I'll tell you, Bob, it's really making me wonder whether this is the same person," Hoyt frowned.

"He'll never be the same person he was when he first started playing this game," Bob lit a cigarette reflectively. "I can damn well guarantee that."

Pastor Matt Mitchell remembered when the beautiful redhead first started attending services at the Force of God Christian Church in Lower Manhattan. He knew she was the one putting $100 bills in the tithe envelope, leaving it unsigned so that he could not send her an end-of-year receipt for her taxes. He noticed that she sang along with the hymns and was very friendly with those sitting next to her at the beginning and end of services. When she left, at first she shook his hand and complimented him on his sermons. After a couple of visits she began hugging him. He was nearly taken aback at being hugged by such a lovely woman, but soon got over it. Eventually he came to realize that the Lord sent her as a genuine addition to the congregation, and praised Him for the blessing.

After a few weeks she remained behind after service and asked him to pray over her. He learned her name was Sabrina Brooks, and she was the heiress of Brooks Chemical Company on Staten Island. She had just lost her father and inherited the family business. She was going through a time of transition and needed the Lord to provide guidance. He prayed with her and asked for the Lord's blessing in this time of trouble. Only a couple of weeks later, she asked if she could come by after Wednesday prayer meeting for counseling.

Matt had opened the storefront church six months earlier on a wing and a prayer. Most of the regulars were people living in the neighborhood and transients from the Bowery. They were waiting to see if he was going to make it work and contributed as best they could. The handful of attendees were curious as to why such a gorgeous lady was coming out to the Bowery at such an hour to attend services here. So was Matt. He was hoping he would get to the bottom of what this was about.

Sabrina was chatty and personable, and they went from small talk to a brief update on how things were going at the BCC. She then began talking about her relationship with her father. She had grown rebellious after her mother's death and grew estranged from him. She switched majors from chemistry to law enforcement and began partying heavily after transferring from NYU to John Jay College of Criminal Justice. She blamed herself for his death from a broken heart and devoted herself to making things right. Only she could not walk away from her dream of law enforcement and tried to make it all happen, to bring it all together.

"Pastor, I've never told anyone what I'm about to tell you. I know there's a clergy-penitent privilege, so you don't have to tell anyone if you don't want to. I know you're a good man, and you'll always do what you think is right," she said with tears flowing down her cheeks.

"I would never betray your confidence," Matt assured her.

"I'm the Nightcrawler."

This set off a wave of mixed emotions inside him, most of which caused him to suspect she was either hallucinating or setting him up for some kind of scam. She then asked him to accompany her out back to the parking area behind the church.

"This is my gear," she popped her trunk, showing him the ninja suit, the SWAT gear and the gas gun. She picked up a modified harpoon and led him over to a three-story building next door. She then fired the spear into the soffit and fascia of the building where it trailed a length of silk rope.

"I'll climb up there for you if it'll convince you. I can do it in ten seconds."

"No, no, I believe you," he managed. She jerked the rope three times, causing the hook to release the line. She pushed a button on a reel which rewound the rope into its spool, leaving the harpoon hidden from sight in the roof overhang.

Thus began one of the strangest episodes of his life. He was immersed in his role as Pastor, working eighteen hours a day in building his Church and supporting its family. Only a part of him was continually praying for Sabrina, searching the Internet for information about the Nightcrawler. He wondered if she was going to meet her end at last, if the police or her enemies had finally caught up with her. Now at last it was over. She was lying in Bellevue in a coma. No one knew if she would ever recover.

He came up once a week and prayed at her bedside for twenty to thirty minutes, patting her hand before leaving. He always stopped to thank Nurse Shakeera for taking care of her.

"I shouldn't say this, but she's my favorite patient," the black girl confided. "She's like my little doll, my special flower. I love doing her hair and putting on her makeup. She's just so beautiful, I can't wait for the day she opens her eyes and I can hear her voice."

"She's very special to a lot of people," Matt's eyes grew misty.

"I know. There's always so many floral arrangements sent up here. Her partner, Mr. Aeppli, lets them stay here for a couple of days before he sends them to the chapel. I tell you, that chapel gonna know when she gone, that's for sure."

Matt continued to wonder whether he should have betrayed her trust and turned her in to the authorities. She would have never forgiven him and he would have never forgiven himself. Still, he knew one thing for sure. She would not be here, in a coma, with no one knowing if she would ever be revived.

He took the long walk to the subway, carrying a terrible burden that only a Christian pastor could bear.

The cause of concern over the Nightcrawler War in Brighton Beach was that it came at such an inopportune time. The Chechens and the Russians had made the peace and were trying to repair the power structure that nearly collapsed during the recent gang wars. Stanislav Lipki had risen to the top of the volcano by default. As a result, he received constant advice from Moscow as to how he needed to assume the posture to fit the role. They expected him to morph from a ruthless drug dealer to a benevolent godfather overnight, and he was doing little to disappoint.

He purchased a four million dollar mansion along the border of Gravesend and Sheepshead Bay that looked a lot like the Corleone home in *The Godfather*. He found a grandmother whose grandchild had been killed by gang violence and paid her $500 weekly to be his maid. He recruited an older man from Odessa to be his caretaker. Lipki was pleased that almost no English was spoken in his new home. He furnished it with tasteful Victorian furniture that gave it the pre-Communist Muscovite atmosphere he desired. After stocking its pantries and cellars with fine wine and delicacies, he felt he truly had a place to call home.

Lipki invited his lieutenants to a sumptuous dinner of beef stroganoff and fried potatoes, with caviar and cheese appetizers and plenty of wine to wash it down with. After dinner they were treated to Cuban cigars and Beluga Noble vodka. The men were in fine spirits and felt little jealousy as Lipki took Max Mironov on a short tour of his new domicile. The strains of traditional Russian music could be heard through state of the art speakers as the two made their way down a long corridor.

"This is my treasure," Lipki stood alongside a draped painting of a nun with a dreamy look on her translucent face. Floodlights enhanced the oil portraiture to make the image seem angelic and almost lifelike.

"I don't know much about art, Mr. Lipki," Max admitted, "but I've got to say that's a beautiful picture. Who painted it?"

"Most experts would agree it is a work by Valentin Serov. It was stolen from a museum outside St. Petersburg by the Nazis before the siege of Leningrad. The Communists recovered it after the war and had it shipped to the Russian Museum, but somehow it never got there. It passed through the hands of a couple of commissars before the collapse of the Soviet Union. It ended up in the collection of a powerful *vor* in Moscow, a man who was one of my father's mentors. The man died recently and had it sent to me."

"That's quite a history," Max said admiringly.

"One of our great traditions is to leave a valued memento behind to someone who will lead our people in the future. This way your memory is cherished by the future leader, who will pass the treasure along to his successor. I will pass this on to someone one day."

"You're still a young man, Mr. Lipki. It will be a long, long time from now."

"The other reason why this is precious to me is because of my mother. She was a grade school teacher and an art lover. If she lived to see me own such a thing, she would consider it my greatest achievement. Not the Family, not the money, not the success. For her, it would have been the knowledge that her son owned a priceless work of art by Serov."

"That's how mothers are, I guess. They see things differently."

"So do fathers. As the father figure of this family, I see things through different eyes than my soldiers. I see different qualities, not just earning ability, or courage, or cunning. I look for things like loyalty and honor. I will build this family on men of loyalty and honor. I will build this family on men like you."

"I'm honored by your words," Max spoke hesitantly. "I'm honored to be here, more than words can say. I…I just wonder. I have to ask you, Mr. Lipki. Why me?"

"You demonstrate your loyalty and honor in your relationship with your friends," Lipki searched his eyes. "You stand by them despite the criticism of your comrades. You defend them even though you know it can cost your opportunities to advance in our ranks. This is a rare quality, especially for one of your age. The question now is: will they prove to be as loyal to you? Would they carry guns to defend you? Would they risk their lives to protect yours?"

"I believe any of them would take a bullet for one another," Max asserted. "That would lead me to believe they would take a bullet for me."

Lipki seemed satisfied as he returned Max to the spacious parlor, and after a few more drinks they retired for the evening. Max called his friends in advance and hightailed it back to the neighborhood where they met at the Coney Island Bar and Grill on Surf Avenue. The sports bar had the atmosphere of a hobbyist biker lounge, which made it easy for the motley crew to melt into the crowd.

"So you're in with the in crowd," Ron grinned as he sipped his dark beer. "Don't make no sense that the big man himself would walk you through his crib if he didn't like you."

"It's not him I'm worried about…well, not so much. It's those goons of his. They're like a pack of bitches looking to scratch the new dog's eyes out."

"I get that every time I check out a new place on Christopher Street," Chuck said slyly, causing the girls to giggle.

"This isn't funny," Max grumbled. "Those bastards're liable to try and set me up. You guys're being careful not to deal in the 'hood, and no new customers, right?"

"The girls on Christopher Street just love it," Chuck cooed. "I go up there with my baggies and exchange them for cash in one trip. No snags on my end."

"I got my buyers in Flatbush who go cash on demand," Ron nodded. "I zip right under the radar past them Rastafarian cowboys out that way. I'm in and out so fast I barely get to finish a drink."

"My connection in the mail room buys me out in one shot," Carissa spoke of her Wall Street job as a bank secretary.

"So do the kids at the phone room where I'm at," Lori agreed.

"Okay, so everybody's cool," Max was reassured. "Let's just turn our scores in on time and make sure he gets every cent of what's owed him. I know they're gonna see how we make up the difference between ounces and grams. That'll be my problem, though. Let's just turn it in as quick as we can and I'll see to it that they go back to kilos and quit jerking us around."

"It shouldn't be a major problem," Carissa insisted. "You can go online and get all kinds of info about metric conversions."

"There's another thing," Max said reluctantly. "That gang of hijackers that tried to rip us off the other day. I didn't say anything to Lipki because I didn't want him to start looking at us funny. I don't want him to think we can't hold our places on the street. It just that he made a remark about my friends being able to back me up. I'm thinking maybe those hijackers have been hitting on the other crews. If they have, and Lipki decides to make a move on them, we may have to stand and be counted. I'm just wondering if you guys would make that kind of commitment."

"Hell, I'm not a hired killer, I'm not gonna carry a gun and put myself in the line of fire for the Russian Mob," Ron shook his head. "Now, if one of us was being threatened, sure I'd be there. I might start packing if I thought there was a crew out there planning to jack us. As far as getting caught up in a gang war, I'm afraid you'd have to count me out. I don't plan on doing no time in Attica for no one."

"I'm with Ron on that," Chuck agreed. "If any one of us was in a jam, you call me and I'm there. But going out on the street for Lipki and the Mafiya, well, that's a long and dangerous one way street. I know they wouldn't piss on me if I caught fire, so why would I get involved?"

"I agree," Carissa joined in. "We all know what male chauvinist pigs those Russians are...no offense, Max, but that's just how it is. Those guys put women, gays and blacks in the same category. If we were a bunch of Guidos from Bensonhurst, they'd be kissing your ass to see if you could help them make some Italian Mob connections."

"That makes it unanimous," Lori said. "Unless you think otherwise."

"Hey, it's all for one and one for all," Max insisted. "That's how it's always been and how it'll always be. We all dropped out of high school together, for god sakes. I just want to be sure that we're willing to back each other up. Lipki asked me about that. He's not going to increase our supply if we cut and run if there's any trouble."

"Well, none of us were gonna run off the other night before the Nightcrawler showed up," Lori replied. "Speaking of which, isn't that your ace in the hole if anything happens?"

"Are you kidding? That vigilante's just using me for a source in keeping tabs on the hood. If he finds out that hijack crew's working in this area again, he'll probably be back. I'm not gonna hold my breath until it happens."

They broke up shortly afterward, and the guys walked the girls to their cars before parting ways to find their own rides. Max noticed that the group was noticeably reticent on the subject of the Nightcrawler. He wondered whether they were communicating amongst themselves about the implications. He knew they were greatly concerned about Lipki's bounty on the vigilante and any possible connections in the hood. He just hoped they hadn't come up with a contingency plan that might not necessarily include him if the spit hit the fan.

He began heading down a dark side street just as a black car with its headlights off swerved sharply alongside the curb near where he was walking. He backed up warily, ready to break into a sprint as the passenger window rolled down.

"Get in," the distorted voice called him.

"You know, you're some piece of work," Max snapped. "How would I know you're not one of those hijackers looking to take me out?"

"I wouldn't be asking you to get in, would I?"

Soon they were cruising along Shore Parkway, heading towards Plum Beach where they were less likely to be noticed by gang members of any affiliation.

"So how're things in Paradise?"

"How should I know? Why don't you drop dead and find out?"

"Excuse me, did I do something to annoy you?"

"Besides letting my friends know we were connected?"

"Look, it was better they found out now before things start heating up. Lipki and the Mafiya know it's not just me they've got a problem with. Those hijackers have been cutting his corners for weeks now. Now your friends know they aren't dependent on Lipki to watch their backs."

"They also know that he'd pay a half million dollars for info leading to chopping them up and dumping them into the ocean."

"It'll make them keep their mouths shut and their ears to the ground. There's a storm coming, and the careful ones are the ones who'll survive."

"Survive? Look, we're dope dealers, it's what we do for a living. We're hooked up with Lipki because he's a reliable source. I didn't join his gang, he absorbed us. Just like I didn't answer any ad looking to team up with no damn Nightcrawler."

"Sometimes it's safer to be in the middle. When you're on one side or the other, there's a winner and a loser. Somebody gets to crash and burn. In the middle you get to pick up the pieces."

"What do you mean, winner and loser? Aren't you on the cops' side? You're one of the good guys. The good guys are supposed to win."

"The cops wear badges. I'm in the middle, same as you."

"The middle? Let me ask you something. Are you a psycho? Did you escape from a mental institution?"

"Something like that."

\* \* \*

Shakeera Smith was in process of changing the linen on the ward and was startled by the sudden appearance of an angry Hoyt Wexford behind her.

"Detective Wexford. How are you today?"

"I've got a couple of questions I want to ask you. Come with me."

She followed him back to Sabrina's bed where he angrily pulled back her sheet and pointed at her left forearm.

"These bruises. How in hell did this happen?"

"I already reported them to Nurse Ratched. They happens sometimes with comatose patients. You ever see that movie *Million Dollar Baby* with Clint Eastwood?"

"How about these?" Hoyt pulled up Sabrina's pajama shirt to reveal bruises on her left side from her breast to her hip. "Did you report these to Minnie too?"

"Well, they's bedsores. We needs to treat them so they don't get infected. Like I said, they had that movie where that girl had her leg amputated because of that."

"You listen to me," Hoyt waved his finger in her face. "If anyone does anything to this woman, I'll burn each and every one of you to the ground. That I swear."

"Now there's no need to go threatening people, Detective. Nobody hiding anything from you. You know there's such things as HIPAA laws and whatnot. Whether this lady's comatose or not don't deprive her of her privacy rights."

"This doesn't look like bedsores. Did you drop her on the floor?"

"Look, you needs to talk to Nurse Ratched. They's lots of issues involved here. She's very light-skinned, which makes her susceptible to bruising. It's also possible we needs to shift her around more, like let her lay on her sides. That can get risky, because we wouldn't want her to lose circulation in her arms or experience breathing problems. She can't exactly tell us whether her arms're going to sleep or she can't breathe right, you know."

"Yeah? Well, get Minnie on the line. We need to talk."

Minnie Ratched was a stone wall awaiting the onslaught of Hoyt Wexford storming her door. She turned from her PC almost as if on cue as the detective loomed over her desk.

"Nurse Ratched, may I have a word?"

"Certainly, Detective. Have a seat."

"I had an intriguing chat with Nurse Smith about the rehabilitation program that Dr. Schumann has implemented for my fiancé. There was mention of the outside chance of amputating her leg."

"I'm quite sure that Nurse Smith was referring to a worst-case scenario that will, in all likelihood, never happen here."

"Nurse Ratched, I don't give a damn about a worst-case scenario or what may never happen. I am not threatening you, I am making a promise. If anything – *anything* –like that happens to Sabrina, there is nothing on earth that will stop me from frying everyone responsible."

"Detective Wexford, are you threatening me?"

"I'm not sure if you're listening to me, Nurse Ratched."

"Should I consult a lawyer?"

"Maybe I should consult Dr. Schumann and cut to the chase here."

"Let me call Dr. Schumann and I'll tell him you're on the way."

Hoyt steamed down the hall to the elevator, and within minutes he was on street level heading for the garage. He peeled rubber down the rampway, and within the hour he parked the car and was on the way to Dr. Schumann's office.

"Detective Wexford," Schumann rose to shake his hand as Hoyt came through the office door. "How nice it is to see you again."

"Did Minnie Ratched give you a heads up?"

"I'm sure it was about Ms. Brooks' rehab program," Schumann folded his hands atop his desk.

"There was mention about a movie called *Million Dollar Baby*. You ever see it?"

"I may have. I'm sure you're familiar with Einstein's theory about brain clutter. If you become distracted with the insignificancies of life, sometimes you lose focus on your life mission. I'm afraid I don't have that convenience."

"Well, let's focus on bedsores, gangrene and amputation."

"The movie you refer to took a bit of a leap as far as real-life scenarios are concerned. You must bear in mind the fact that the Brooks Foundation has taken great precautions to ensure that such oversights are avoided in this case."

"And who is the Brooks Foundation?"

"I'm a doctor, Detective Wexford."

"Tell me about the precautions."

"Well, we are adopting different strategies and attempting different methods in expediting Ms. Brooks' rehabilitation. One thing we are doing is manipulating her joints and limbs to prevent atrophy. As an athlete, I am sure that you realize that even the involuntary flexing of a muscle results in stimulation."

"Yeah. So?"

"If we flex and unflex her arms and legs, we may be forestalling the atrophic process. We have also considered the use of electro-stimulation."

"What do you mean, shocking her?"

"Not in such a sense that you may think. I'm sure that you are aware that the neural system is predicated on electron stimuli in the form of brain waves. The theory is that light stimulation can invigorate the muscles, reversing the stagnation of progressive atrophy."

"So is this standard practice? I mean, does Bellevue…"

"You must remember that Bellevue is a State hospital, in every sense of the term. They have their protocol that they are forbidden to circumvent. In

Ms. Brooks' case, we are implementing certain procedures outside of Bellevue's protocols."

"So you admit you're operating outside of Bellevue's standard procedures."

"Let me put it this way, Detective," Schumann took off his glasses and set them on the desk before him. "We can cease and desist from our rehab schedule at your insistence. If you choose to pursue this, you will be surrendering Ms. Brooks to the hospital's standard operating procedure. I doubt that they will be taking any alternative courses to enhance your fiancé's rehabilitation outside of their protocol."

"So, no flex approach or shock treatment."

"We can cancel or curtail at your request. We never had any desire to operate outside of the law. Perhaps we did not consult Bellevue's administrative staff, but it was never our intent…"

"Look, I won't stand your way. All I ask is that you remain honest with me. You know, transparency. I saw black and blues on her arm and her side and I was concerned."

"So should you be. All we ask is that you work together with us, Detective Wexford. Please feel free if you see or suspect anything that is not right with you. Point it out to Nurse Ratched and I guarantee you she will have the answers that you seek."

Hoyt returned to his vehicle afterward and immediately speed-dialed Bob Methot.

"Hey. What's up?"

"You remember Dale Vosberg?"

"Yeah, King of the Dead Zone. What about him?"

"Can you reach out to him? I need a favor."

"Costs money, my friend. Otherwise he's a man you don't want to owe favors to. If he needs to cash in a marker, chances are you'll pay a price you'll never forget."

"That's a non-issue. Make the connection."

"All right. I'll call you this evening."

Hoyt Wexford knew he would be selling a piece of his soul to the Devil, but as he said, price was a non-issue.

He was going to Ground Zero with the Brooks Foundation.

# Chapter Six

Chuck Focker became the one hundred thousandth confirmed victim of Ebola in New York City. He was admitted to Long Island College Hospital at eight AM after showing symptoms of the virus. He tested positive and became another name on the list of patients waiting for vaccine to be delivered to the beleaguered facility. Lori was the first of his friends to learn what happened, and she met with them at Max's apartment that evening to commiserate.

"What do they mean, a waiting list?" Max fumed when he heard the news. "They've got some of the biggest companies in the richest countries in the world working on the vaccine, and there's not enough to go around?"

"I betcha if some rich white dude or his family got sick, there'd be more than enough," Ron shook his head. "They just don't have enough to spare for a gay male. You bet your bottom dollar if a black man or a middle class woman catches that virus, we don't get none either."

"You know, there's been rumors on the Internet that the gangs have been jacking supply trucks carrying the vaccines and selling them on the black market," Lori pointed out. "The City's been covering it up so the cops don't catch all that heat."

"You don't suppose those hijackers that've been hitting Lipki's network might have…" Carissa held her hand to her lips. "Oh my gosh. They're not just hurting Lipki, they're endangering the lives of thousands of innocent people."

"Max, the Nightcrawler is your friend, and if you ask me, I don't think he's doing enough," Lori flared. "He's supposed to be this hot-shot superhero. I think he would know if those hijackers were ripping off medical supplies for Ebola victims."

"What?" Max stared incredulously, wiggling his finger in his ear. "I can't believe what I'm hearing. Are you selling dope or using it up yourself? The Nightcrawler is a psychopath. When did I ever tell you he was my friend? He can come back here and kill me any time he wants. Why don't you stay here a couple of nights until he comes by, and you can voice your opinion then."

"The part I don't understand is why he's been coming to you for information," Ron mused. "What are you giving him? Are you dropping a dime on Lipki?"

"We already went over this!" Max stared back and forth from Ron to Carissa. "Are you seriously listening to her? You think I have any say in what the Nightcrawler does?"

"Our friend is lying up sick in that hospital," Ron said quietly. "Maybe the Nightcrawler could make a difference."

"You people are messed up! What am I supposed to do? 'Uh, say, Mr. Nightcrawler, my friends think you aren't doing enough to combat the Ebola plague. Do you think you can drop what you're with Lipki and look around to see if you can find any Ebola vaccine hijackers?' "

"Sure, go ahead, make a joke of it," Carissa said accusingly. "It's not you lying up there in Long Island College Hospital dying of Ebola. If it was you, I know Chuck would try and help."

"That's it! You're serious! Wait, I can handle this! Let me get up and see if I can pull one of those hijack trucks out of my ass!"

"You see, Max, you're turning into a Russian gangster," Lori was morose. "Everything's a big joke with you these days."

"I don't need this crap," Max hopped off the couch and yanked his leather jacket off the rack, storming out the door. "Ron, go ahead and lock up when you leave. I'm going for a ride and get some air. The air in here stinks like bull crap."

"Yeah, well, you'd better hold your nose, because it's coming out of your mouth," Lori retorted before he slammed the door behind him.

He began walking towards Mc Donald Avenue, not caring who was out there or who saw him. He knew there was the ever-present danger of running into a homeless person carrying the virus. There was also the chance of coming across rival gangsters, or dope addicts who knew he might be carrying. He didn't care right now. He was so mad he would've thrown down with a cop if one tried to roust him. He felt like everyone had gone open season on him, and he wasn't taking anymore. Not off his friends, or the Lipkis, or even the damn Nightcrawler. No more.

Only when he turned down Avenue U, he perceived a scuffle coming from an alleyway between one of the brownstones and decided to investigate. No matter how crap went down, the 'hood was still the 'hood. Neighbors watched each other's back, plain and simple. Everyone was related to someone. The older guy was somebody's grandpa, the next guy had a wife and kids, the teen kid was somebody's son. And you always defended a Russian woman from the cradle to the grave. Lipki himself would break your legs if he found out you didn't.

As he approached the alley he noticed a truck parked alongside the entryway. It was one of Polski's Sausage trucks, the kind that took the runs down to the Carolinas to bring back cigarettes. If you bought boxloads of cartons directly from the wholesalers, you avoided the Federal tax and scored thousands of bucks at resale.

It was one of Lipki's more lucrative rackets and someone was trying to swipe the meat right off his plate.

He peered into the shadows and saw four black-clad gunmen with flashlight beams darting to and fro. One stood over Zbigniew Polski, who sat cowering on the muddy pavement.

"Where'd you throw those keys, you stupid son of a bitch?" one of the hi-jackers snarled. "If I don't find them in two minutes your ass'll suck wind!"

"You better get out of here now while you still have a chance!" Polski cried. "If they catch you looking inside my truck they will kill you!"

"Hey!" Max yelled as he stood at the edge of the alley, partly hidden by the brick corner. "This is Nightcrawler territory! I just texted the Nightcrawler, he'll be here in two minutes! You better haul ass if you know what's good for you!"

"Nightcrawler!" they began swearing and cursing. "That dirty rat called the Nightcrawler!"

At once they began charging up the alley, one of them kicking Polski in the face as he raced by. Max darted away from the entrance and hid behind the truck as they began scurrying towards their getaway SUV. Within seconds they leaped into their vehicle and sped off towards Coney Island Avenue.

"Thank god you came along. Thank you, my friend," Polski said as he wiped the mud from his face, helped to his feet by Max. "But why did you call the Nightcrawler? He is worse than the police. He burn one of our trucks!"

"I lied," Max admitted. "Lucky thing they went for it. Come on, let's bring this truck in. I'll call Vitali and tell him what happened. He'll have his whole crew out waiting for us."

About a half hour later, they arrived at Lipki's warehouse on Shore Boulevard. The street was dotted with four-man teams that could have been mistaken for guys hanging out if it were not well after 2 AM. Polski pulled up in front of the warehouse as the steel overhead door was rolled up. Max hopped out of the passenger side and was met at once by Vitali.

"What happened, *malchik*?" Vitali ribbed him. "Needed someone to hold your hand?"

"The hijackers nearly lifted this whole load," Max shot back. "If I hadn't come along, the *bugor* would've been a little light in the pocket this week."

"The *bugor* would hardly come up short if just one of his loads were lifted," Vitali sneered. "Just as he would barely notice the take from a *goluboy* go missing from the till."

"You know, I can't do anything about the *bugor* talking about my friends. I'm not so sure it applies to you."

"You seem to be feeling pretty strong. You think bringing in this truck is going to support so much weight?"

"I only hope that it will keep the *bugor* from stepping into the midst of a private dispute."

"Come now, let us put these petty rivalries aside," Yuri came forth as the two gangsters stepped into each other's airspace. "The *bugor* wants us to join arms in this thing. My car is waiting. Let us drive to his home, he is expecting us."

Max reluctantly got into the back seat of Yuri's SUV alongside Vitali, and was even more apprehensive as his brother Timur slipped into the passenger seat. He was ready to throw open the door and dive out onto the asphalt if the car did not proceed in the direction of Lipki's mansion in Gravesend. To his relief, they proceeded along the appropriate thoroughfares and wound up in front of the stately manor.

"Welcome, my friends," Lipki awaited them in the foyer as two bodyguards the size of pro wrestlers escorted them along the threshold. They had been followed by the Grozny brothers, who closely followed the Explorer in their Mercedes-Benz. Max was not comforted by the knowledge they had been escorted by the Groznys, but Lipki's greeting put him somewhat more at ease.

"I am glad that you could all come here at such short notice. As you know, we are having to deal with these outsiders who seek to disrupt the way of things here in our community. Yet there are other things happening that will restore the balance and order of everything. Our friends the Chechens are preparing a stew that the Americans will choke on. Fear not, my comrades. These things are happening as we speak."

"Are we not all Americans?" Max could not help himself.

"America is a stewpot," Lipki raised his hand dramatically, evoking a laugh from Vitali, Timur, Pyotr and Nestor. "All the races come here and mix amongst each other, producing new breeds of American mongrels. Only we Russians remain pure, or at least the Russians who respect their race and their heritage, their tradition. It is good to be American, to enjoy our Constitutional rights. Only we must remain strong. The law is an instrument used by the rich and powerful, just as it is in mother Russia. The Mafiya is the alternative for those who have no protection from the law. This is how it has always been, this is how it will always be."

"I understand this, my *bugor.*"

"We do not try to choose your friends for you, Max," Lipki said gently. "We only ask that you choose your friends carefully. Honorable men associate with honorable men. People seek their own kind, it is a law of nature. The blacks gravitate towards other blacks, the gays reside alongside other gays. Women seek solace among other women. This group of yours, it is an unnatural mix. I do not tell you how to live your life, my friend. I only ask that you exercise caution. When all is said and done – at the end of the day, as they say – the only ones who will stand for you through thick and thin are your own people, your kinsmen, the Russians."

"I respect your advice, and I do not question your judgment. I only feel that a man is without honor when he turns his back on his friends."

"And I will never ask you to do so. Just be on guard, my friend. Our enemies are everywhere. Be vigilant, and stay close. Do not stray so far that the enemy catches you unprotected."

"I'm keeping my eyes wide open. We all are. Believe me, if they catch any of us they'll have hell to pay. We're watching each other's back, and we're here whenever you need us."

"I know I can count on you, my friend," Lipki patted his shoulder reassuringly. Max felt as if a hundred pounds just fell from his back.

Shortly after Max left the apartment, his three friends departed shortly thereafter. Ron lived near Bensonhurst and headed in the opposite direction from Carissa and Lori. The girls soon parted ways and Lori was scurrying towards her apartment building when a car pulled up and double-parked near where she was walking.

"Say, Miss," the passenger called to her, "we're looking for Surf Avenue. You know which way Surf Avenue is?"

"No speak English," she called back, picking up her pace.

At once the car doors swung open and two men emerged from the back seats, breaking into a dash straight towards Lori. She started to scream but was grabbed and thrown onto the hood of the car next to where they were idling.

"Okay, bitch. We know you're dealing dope around here. Tell us where your connection's holed up and we'll let you go."

Lori struggled against her assailants but her strength failed in a short time. She was in her late twenties but had spent far too much time smoking weed and drinking beer than she had back in her high school days when she permanently bonded with Max and the gang. She had been somewhat athletic back them, but cigarettes and alcohol had taken their toll. She was still a good-looking woman but her strength and endurance were not what they used to be. She didn't know how much pain she could endure. If they tried to beat the information out of her she was not sure if she could hold out.

"I don't know what you're talking about! Let me go or I'll call the cops!"

"You drug-dealing skank, they'll haul your ass out to Atlantic Avenue and put you in a cage. Give up your supplier and we let you walk."

"Don't call me a skank! Your mother's a skank!" she kicked her heels against the car bumper.

"All right, this is your last chance," she heard a metallic snapping sound. "Give us the address or I cut your hooters off and throw them in the street."

"Go cut your mother's hooters, you son of a bitch," she struggled even harder.

"Okay," they pulled her wrists and ankles until she was spread-eagled. "You asked for it."

She started to scream before a resounding thump caused the entire vehicle to shake. She twisted around and realized they had relaxed their grip upon her. She looked up and saw the body of a redheaded woman sprawled across the roof of the car.

"Holy crap!" one of them exclaimed. "It's a dead woman!"

"That's not just *any* dead woman! It's Deadwoman! Let's get the hell outta here!"

Lori was winded from her struggles, and feebly rolled onto her side to get a better view of the fallen woman. She looked up and saw the titian tresses flowing down over the windshield, cracked from the force of the woman's fall. Lori shoved herself up onto all fours and leaned toward the woman, trying to get a glimpse of the face shrouded by the thick red hair.

"Are you okay?" Lori managed. "You saved my life. Can you hear me? Let's get out of here. I'll help you come down from there."

She rose up on her knees and reached up, gingerly reaching towards the woman's face and touching her crimson locks. As she leaned toward the woman, at once the eyes popped open and fixed a terrifying stare on Lori. She gasped with fright and started to pull away, only Deadwoman reached out and grabbed her wrist. Lori let out a hysterical scream and wrenched away with all her might. Only the momentum caused her to tumble backwards and slide off the hood, landing on her behind on the asphalt.

Lori rolled to her feet and began staggering away, weeping with fright as she trotted down the street. She reached the corner just as two squad cars cut off her path, arriving from opposite directions. She sank to her knees, sobbing piteously as the officers emerged from the car and took her into custody.

Hoyt Wexford arrived at Dale Vosberg's shipping container a couple of hours before Lori was arrested. It sat on a nearly-deserted pier along the East River in Lower Manhattan. The storage area was fenced off and weeds surrounded the rickety chain link fence. Rusty barbed wire drooped from the top posts, and a thick rusted chain served to keep the front gate closed. It had no lock, for no one in the neighborhood would think of approaching this place in their wildest dreams.

The door to the container was slightly off its hinges and shrieked loudly when opened. There were a couple of extension cords running from a generator that provided illumination from hanging light bulbs. The floors were rubber-matted much like a workout room. Plywood provided framing along the walls, and from these hung a sizeable tool collection. Only there were what appeared to be instruments of torture among them which Hoyt found disturbing. There was a wooden table near the far wall, speckled with what resembled dried blood.

"I thought those things were illegal."

Vosberg never turned or looked up as Hoyt entered. He focused his bi-focaled gaze intently on the double-barreled Mossberg shotgun he had sawed the barrel off and was filing down. He wore a white wife-beater t-shirt and black pants along with black socks and $100 dress shoes. He sat on a stool alongside a workbench where a hacksaw and other tools were scattered.

"So I hear."

"Planning on using it anytime soon?"

"Nah. Some gangbanger wants to buy it. Stupid bastard's planning to use shells loaded with dimes. Saw it in a movie. Dimes don't do half the damage that double-ought shot does."

"Did you tell him?"

"Hell no. I hope it blows up in his face."

There was a long pause.

"You get to check that thing out for me?"

"Yeah."

Another pause. The only sound in the room was that of Vosberg's file.

"What'd you come up with?"

"It's all off-shore stuff," Vosberg put down the shotgun and the file, standing up and stretching before retrieving his Marlboros and lighter from the tabletop. He offered one to Hoyt, who graciously declined.

"That's what I'd figured."

"Way off-shore. If I didn't know better I'd think it was money laundering. They've got five dummy companies who are running the cash through an account in Cuba. That's a stone wall in most cases. I got through that, but found out it runs back into Sinaloa in Mexico. That's cartel country. Whoever's running that Brooks Foundation did a lot of homework and made some serious connections."

"Sabrina couldn't have possibly set something up like that. Neither could Jon Aeppli," Hoyt ran his fingers through his hair. "It had to be the board members."

"Here's the list of names and the chain of command I came up with," Vosberg picked up a small manila packet and handed it to Hoyt. "I had some reliable friends in Boca Raton and Houston do the footwork on this. We got twelve names, and ten of them are either aliases or completely bogus. This whole set-up looks like a vinyl siding company."

"Who are the legit names?"

"Brooks and Aeppli, who did you think?"

"This is insane," Hoyt stared at the wall. "Sabrina's in a coma and Jon's spending over twelve hours a day supervising that Ebola project. Who the hell's running that Foundation, a bunch of ghosts?"

"Maybe that Deadwoman character they've got running with the Nightcrawler."

"Yeah," Hoyt managed a smile. "You should see the cartoons those jokers at OCU are leaving in our Nightcrawler Squad room."

"Could be that's who you should be checking out," Vosberg blew a stream of smoke to one side. "You might kill two birds with one stone."

"Kill two birds. That's a good one."

"You want me to look at those nurses and that doctor?"

"No," Hoyt frowned. "Not just yet. Right now Sabrina's wellbeing depends on them. They're already sticking their necks out for her. If they thought I was prying into their personal lives they might quit taking chances in providing her treatment."

"What do you mean? Are they experimenting on her?"

"No, I'd call it more holistic than anything. Dr. Schumann already explained it to me. If Bellevue's administrative staff got wind of it they might make a move on Schumann. I don't want that to happen. I think Schumann is Sabrina's best chance for recovery. I'll just leave him alone for now."

"Okay. If you want me to look at him just let me know."

"How much do I owe you?"

"You owe me a favor, that's all," Vosberg peered over his glasses. "No big deal. I heard all about your fiancé and what happened to her. I just hope she gets better. I wish you all the luck."

"Thanks, Dale," the men shook hands before Hoyt took his leave.

Hoyt stared glumly into the shadowy New York harbor before slipping back into his Camry. Sometimes he found it all so depressing, he didn't know where to turn. He couldn't understand why men like Dale Vosberg were a necessary evil. He wondered whether there were any good guys left in the world. Before he at least had Bree to turn to, but now she seemed to be slipping away from him. He could not help but feel as if the Brooks Foundation had a tighter grip on her than he ever would. If it came to a showdown between him and Dr. Schumann, he was starting to wonder who would come out on top.

"Hey, kid."

He answered his cell phone and could hear that Bob Methot had been drinking. Instead of slurring, his voice took on a cutting edge after a few rounds.

"Yeah. Just got done seeing Vosberg."

"Well, something else just came up. They got some crazy broad in lockdown who wants to make a deal. They called me because she was mentioning the Crawler and Deadwoman. She also says she has some intel on the Brighton hijackers. She says if we put her under protection and let her walk she'll give up everything."

His heart was pounding as he sailed across the Brooklyn Bridge en route to Atlantic Avenue. At last he had a chance to confront someone who had come face-to-face with the impostor, not just having gotten pounded by him. It was also his opportunity to learn about the female corpse that was acting as a decoy for the impostor. He knew that apprehending the impostor would get the cops off Bree's trail. The black suits around Bellevue would disappear, and even Kelly Stone would return to Washington admitting that the Nightcrawler case was closed.

Hoyt arrived at the Brooklyn House of Detention twenty minutes later, parking in the garage on Court Street before walking down to the cloistered facility. He took the elevator to the interview room where Bob, Jerry and Don were on the other side of the two-way mirror watching a detective asking Lori Murphy a bunch of routine questions.

"Here's her rap sheet, nothing that'd raise an eyebrow," Jerry handed Hoyt a clipboard. "There's a possession of marijuana, a drunk and disorderly, and possession of a deadly weapon. She spent the night here after each bust and got off with probation. We don't really have anything on her this time. She has a half gram of China White. They'll let her walk. She's more worried about who may be waiting for her to get out."

"She said she met the Nightcrawler?"

"She says her crew made a deal with him. She also says this wasn't her first run in with the hijackers."

"C'mon, Bob, let's go hit her up," Hoyt said as he headed for the vestibule.

Lori was stressed out, her pretty green eyes staring wildly as the two detectives relieved their colleague. Her Styrofoam cup of coffee sat between her arms, stretched across the table as they noticed her white-knuckled fists tapping impatiently upon the metallic surface.

"So what, are you guys in charge here?"

"We can help cut to the chase," Hoyt sat down across from her as Bob leaned against the wall to her left. "Have you met the Nightcrawler?"

"No, but he rescued us from the hijackers a few weeks ago. He's got a deal with one of my friends. My friend gives him tips on the Russian gangs and he watches my friend's back."

"So your friend met the Nightcrawler," Hoyt pulled out his Blackberry. "Who's your friend?"

"Slow down, big guy. You haven't even bought me a drink yet."

"Want another coffee?"

"Sure. But you know what I mean. You gotta get me outta Brighton."

"For what? The cops got a call about a disturbance and picked you up running down the street, screaming bloody murder at two in the morning. They found a vandalized car and no witnesses. It looked like you did a moonsault on some poor soul's vehicle and got caught running away. Funny thing, you don't look that drunk."

"You know I'm not drunk," she blazed. "The hijackers jumped me on my way home. They wanted me to rat out my friend and were gonna cut me if I didn't talk. Deadwoman saved me, she jumped on that car and scared them off. Only she scared the hell out of me and that's when I lost it. It was a combination of getting attacked and her scaring me. I never get hysterical, you can ask anyone who knows me. Look, imagine you saw somebody lying dead on top of a car, then all of a sudden jumping up and grabbing your arm. You'd piss your pants."

"So what does she look like, the Deadwoman?"

"She's around my size. She has long red hair, and she's kind of big around the top – you know. Real light-skinned, like a dead woman."

"So you got her specs off the Internet," Bob taunted her. "There's about ten websites that have all kinds of descriptions by eyewitnesses who saw the Dead-woman."

"Yeah? Well, she's got bright green eyes, like emeralds. And she's got a little turned-up nose, like a leprechaun or a pixie or something. And she's got full lips, not thin or anything. I bet you don't know anyone else who's seen her face like I have. A lot of people think she's a mannequin. Let me tell you, she's no mannequin."

"You never turned around to see if she was chasing you?" Hoyt asked, the description sending a chill down his spine.

"Look, what did I just tell you? Four guys grab me off the street at two in the morning, hold me down on top of a car and tell me they're gonna cut me. All of a sudden a woman falls out of the sky onto the roof of the car. It scared the guys off. I try to help her and she jumps up and grabs my arm. I ran for my life. What do you mean, did I look to see if she was chasing me? Are you nuts?"

"We'll ask the questions," Bob growled. "So what makes you think the Brighton hijackers were the ones who jumped you? There's plenty of crews chewing on the Russians' turf – the Colombians, the Mexicans, the Jamaicans, Salvadorans, you name it. The hijackers are big game hunters, they aren't gonna waste their time on street trash like you and your friends. Most likely you got jacked by some low-level punks like yourself trying to grab your stash."

"I told you, we got jumped by the hijackers before and the Nightcrawler saved us. It's the same guys, and I got proof."

"What kind of proof?" Hoyt asked.

"Why, are you gonna protect me?"

"You're not worth our time," Bob pushed off the wall truculently. "You won't give us your friend's name because he's a bottom-feeder. You probably came across the hijackers at the same time as the Nightcrawler, and your friend made it sound like the Crawler was watching his back. That friend of yours is a low-life dope dealer who's got you suckered into thinking he's someone important. C'mon, Hoyt, let's get out of here, I'll buy you a beer at O'Keefe's before they close."

"No, wait!" she nearly rose from her seat. "If I give up my friend you got to cut him a deal too. He's in tight with the Grozny brothers. If I say anything I don't want him to get hurt."

"What Grozny brothers?" Bob asked derisively.

"Pyotr and Nestor. Quit jacking me around."

There was a short silence.

"Okay," Hoyt said softly. "So your friend's been dropping dimes on the Groznys. Did you actually meet the Nightcrawler?"

"No, but I saw him up close, about as close as he is to me."

"Yeah?" Bob asked. "What'd he look like?"

"He's not as big as they say. He's about your size. He talks like one of those people with throat cancer, you know, like through a voice box. He had a gun but he never pulled it out. A big gun, like a sawed-off shotgun. Only it was in a side holster. He lowered himself on a rope, like they do in the movies. When they saw him he took off. I was kinda surprised, but you know those stories about that gas of his. I guess they didn't want to take their chances."

"Hey, she hasn't told us one thing we couldn't have gotten off the Internet," Bob sneered. "C'mon, we're wasting our time."

"Yeah?" Lori was contentious. "Well, one of the hijackers started pushing me around. I lifted his wallet."

"*Sure* you did," Bob resumed leaning against the wall.

"Yeah, so?" Hoyt asked. "Where's the wallet?"

"You give me something in writing that you'll get me and my friends out of Brighton, and I'll give you his driver's license."

"What, like a notarized document?" Hoyt chuckled.

"No, just an agreement, like you do with Mafia guys. Come on, dude, you know what I mean."

"Hey, there's a hidden camera, since you know so much. And the guys running it aren't gonna renege on any deals we make or don't make," Bob pointed out.

"Okay," she put her purse on the table and dug out a card, tossing it to Hoyt. He stared at it, feeling the goose bumps again before he handed it to Bob.

"We're gonna keep you overnight, then we'll turn you over to the Sheriff's Department. They'll get you across the river to New Jersey," Hoyt relented. "You give us your friends' names and we'll pick them up. We'll keep you under wraps long enough for us to check this out. If we make any arrests, we'll go from there."

"Just one thing. You got to do right by my Russian friend. The Groznys are crazy, they'll kill his family. Everybody knows it. They killed his friend Tamerlan a few months ago. You pull him out so nobody knows."

"Tamerlan?" Hoyt squinted. "Tamerlan Chekhov?"

"Yeah," she said uncertainly. "It was in the papers."

"Can your friend connect the Groznys to Tamerlan?"

"Yeah, but he won't. Look, I'm giving you the hijackers. You can't go squeezing my friend. The Groznys are psychotic. They cut people's heads off and dump them in the river. They bring the heads with them to drinking parties. You can't put my friend in that position."

"Give us names, we'll get them off the street," Bob gave her the clipboard and a pen.

Lori began writing.

The detectives had been unable to locate Max Mironov. He had been se-questered along with the other core members of the Lipki Gang in their boss' Gravesend mansion. Lipki had a special mission mandated from Moscow, and he would take no chances that any one of them might be delayed or made un-able to attend. His six soldiers had to double up in the three guest bedrooms at the mansion. Max knocked down more than a couple of shots in Lipki's parlor so he had as little conversation with Yuri Kurskov as possible before retiring.

They drove an SUV to their destination in the garment district of Manhattan. Vitali Yakov had not been given the address of directions until a half hour before their departure. Max was given a Glock-17 with a seventeen-round clip holding 9mm shells. He had never pointed a gun at anyone in his life, let alone having fired one. He was no stranger to guns, but every time he had been urged to carry one it came to no consequence. He had no idea what was about to go down here. All he knew was that the Groznys were told they had to provide backup at an important sitdown. His stomach was knotted with worry over the prospects that might lie ahead.

They pulled up across the street from the Akhty Clothing Company on 27$^{th}$ Street off Broadway, and they realized that there were a couple of other SUVs already out front.

"You don't think we're late?" Timur was concerned as his brother Vitali parked the van.

"Not unless my watch is running backwards," Vitali growled. "Let's just get inside and figure out what we're supposed to be doing here."

"Just keep your mouth shut and your eyes open," Pyotr Grozny said as he exited the SUV. "I'll call the shots when we get inside. Our contact may or may not already be here. Just hang loose and look tough. No eating or drinking, don't touch anything. We're here for business. The sooner it's over and the quicker we can get out of here, the better it is for everyone."

"What, not even a glass of water?" Yuri scowled.

"Suppose it's drugged?" Pyotr shot back. "Look, if anything goes sideways in there and I catch a bullet because you didn't have my back, you won't have to worry about Lipki getting hold of you. I'll be the one fixing your ass."

"Screw you," Yuri flipped him off.

The six men crossed the street and found the side door next to the dark-ened storefront ajar. They trudged up the stairs and heard commotion inside the upper room. Pyotr led the way in and they found themselves in a barren showroom. Two long tables had been placed alongside each other, and chairs were positioned on either side. They were taken aback to see that the people in the room were all black.

"Our friends have arrived," the lone woman in the room spoke as her companions turned to stare at the Russians. "Welcome. We will begin just as soon as your leader arrives."

"There is no need for further delay. Let us begin."

Everyone but the woman stood in awe at the sight of the giant stepping through the far door on the opposite side of the room. He stood nearly seven feet tall, clad in a metallic blue armored suit. He wore a helmet with a T-shaped opening that shielded his features entirely. They had all seen the terrorist known as Apollyon on TV and were startled to be seeing him standing before them. The blacks knew he was coming but were still unnerved at his sheer presence.

"It is good to see you again, my friend," Chakra Khan came over and hugged him. Even though she was an amazon standing nearly six and a half feet tall in her heels, she was still dwarfed by the giant weighing nearly three hundred pounds.

"We have advanced rapidly," he remarked. "The name of Boko Haram appears in the news daily. New Yorkers may not have embraced you as a new religion, but they certainly have made no progress in shutting you down."

"Yes, we have taken great strides in bringing new converts into the fold and strengthening our position," she agreed as he joined her at the table. "I believe we have reached the stage where we can put Phase II into effect."

"Most certainly," Apollyon agreed. "The Americans believe we were thwarted by the Nightcrawler when the infidel prevented us from attacking Wall Street. This next move will spread greater terror throughout this nation than the attack on 9/11."

"Praise Allah. We are certain that the results of your mission will plunge the City into utter chaos. It will facilitate our efforts in generating income for Phase III which is approaching very soon."

"Retrieve the item I have left by the door," Apollyon turned to the Russians.

"Go on," Pyotr nudged Max.

He headed to the entrance and found a metal suitcase that he proceeded to bring to the table. It was somewhat heavy and he figured it to be about thirty pounds. He placed it on the table and realized that, at 5'7", he stood shoulder-high to Chakra and Apollyon. They thanked him as he quickly withdrew to rejoin his comrades.

"That is 1.5 million dollars' worth of China White," Apollyon announced. "It is what was left from Tryzub's supply in Brighton Beach. Alexander Malkin told his associates in Dagestan exactly where it was stored. The information was passed along to me. This is heroin cut with methylfentanyl and is extremely addictive. Once cut for street distribution, it will double in weight and value. It should provide Boko Haram with the money needed to put Phase III into effect. Three million dollars buys lots of guns and explosives."

"The new Ebola strain will be too much for this City to bear, my brother," Chakra smiled. "It will be in no shape to stop the wave of terror we will unleash."

"Good," Apollyon rose to leave. "The next phase of the operation will commence within forty-eight hours. Once the people of Manhattan are stricken with the plague, it will be your cue to begin the distribution of China White throughout Upper Manhattan and the South Bronx."

The twelve blacks in the room were astonished by the sight of the heroin, more than any had ever seen in their lives. They also glanced over the Russians and each other. Six of the men were top lieutenants of the 137th Street Gang, and the other six were Nigerians from Boko Haram. They were as leery of each other as of the white men, but none were so foolish as to risk the wrath of Chakra Khan. It was well known that she had ordered over two dozen murders since arriving in East Harlem.

"Excellent," Chakra came around the table to exchange hugs with the masked giant. He disappeared through the far door just as abruptly as he came, and the blacks left in two groups down the main stairwell. Chakra took her leave before the last group departed. The Russians waited until the cars downstairs drove off before exiting the building and heading back towards the BQE.

The car was noticeably silent on the way back to Coney Island. Each man was lost in his own thoughts, and none were overly optimistic about the foreseeable future as being predicted by Apollyon and Chakra Khan.

"You know," Max was unable to control his tongue, "I don't see why Lipki couldn't have cut loose a couple of kis for my crew and see what we could've done with it. With that kinda money, we could move in next to the Jews on the beach, create a little distance from the 'hood. You know, not having to be looking over our shoulders for hijackers wouldn't be so bad..."

"What do you think?" Vitali was unusually inimical. "You don't think any of us wouldn't want a nice place in some condominium? You don't think I'd like to be living down the block from Lipki? I'm no happier about him handing the deal over to the niggers than anybody else. Problem is that it's bigger than Brighton. You saw that guy Apollyon on TV. He's got some super Ebola bomb he's threatening to hit the city with. Homeland Security's gonna be in the 'hood like stink on crap after that. The niggers'll be making the score, and we'll be taking the rap."

"I keep having this dream about the Nightcrawler," Yuri spoke up glumly. "He's got one of our guys, and we blow our guy away to get to him. Then he hits us with the gas and gets away. Again and again, over and over."

"What's it mean?" Max asked.

"It's like we stop at nothing, we sacrifice our own, and we still lose. Nothing changes," Yuri said softly. "After a while it all seems meaningless."

"Hell, I'd take a bullet if it meant whacking the Crawler," Timor grunted.

"Yeah? And when you came around I'd rap you across the teeth," Vitali chastised his younger brother. "Bullets these days, they make holes so big you end up bleeding to death no matter where you get hit."

"He's right," Max spoke up again. "No one should ever get hit. Nobody needs to take a bullet just to make a couple of bucks."

"You take a bullet when your honor's at stake, your respect," Pyotr was emphatic. "When you go out, when you die, that's the most important thing you leave behind. A man can die without a dime to his name, but they remember him forever if he's a man of respect."

"I want both. You die successful if you have both," Max insisted.

"We'll get ours, don't you worry," Nestor assured him. "Look, maybe the Crawler stopped him on Broadway, but he's still got two bombs left. He told them that on TV, they play it every day on cable. If he sets off that bomb, you don't think they'll pay him the ransom to turn over the last one? That one hundred million's gonna trickle down, my friends. You heard his accent, he's Chechen. That gang of theirs, the Tryzub, they made the peace with the Mafiya. They'll give the Mafiya a big cut, and we'll get ours. Lipki won't forget us being here tonight."

"Maybe that's what Lipki wanted us to see," Timor decided. "The blacks will be pushing dope on the street to make their money, trying to dodge every cop and Federal agent out there after that bomb goes off. If everything goes right, all we do is sit back and collect."

*Yeah*, thought Max.

*Exactly what Lipki wanted us to see.*

"You know, the reason why I made Lieutenant over twenty years is not only because of experience. It's because I never lost my suspicion. I considered everyone a suspect until someone was proven guilty. I never stop asking questions, and neither should you."

"Well, that's why I'm here."

"Maybe you asking the *wrong* questions," Leroy Chandler insisted. "What makes you think somebody didn't put that little tramp up to it? They get some intel on a upwardly-mobile young detective, come up with some phony ID, then use it as leverage. Like a seesaw. It lifts them up and lowers him down."

"Sometimes questions get pumped up until they become conspiracy theories," Hoyt retorted. "That's just a neighborhood lass, she's got no real connections outside of her little drug dealing clique. Look, I *know* she saw Deadwoman the other night. She told me things she couldn't have known if she hadn't. Why would've she held onto that ID until now? If she wanted to put the squeeze on Sciaraffo she would've done it a long time ago. Look, she was scared stiff the hijackers were gonna take her out. She held onto that card as her ace in the hole. She didn't tell anyone, not her clique, no one."

"That's her story."

"It's the truth. I know it."

"So you want to meet Sciaraffo?"

"Yeah, I'd like to."

"You know, you already met him over at O'Keefe's that time."

"I figured those fellows were doing some heavy lifting somewhere. I didn't make them for the Brighton hijackers."

"I never mentioned the hijackers, and you'd better not either."

"So you know about this."

"So does Chief Madden. You and your team stumbled across a major undercover operation. Men have put their lives on the line to make this happen. You can ask your questions, but I won't guarantee Robert will answer them. And whatever you hear in that room stays in that room."

"Which room is that?"

"He should be hitting the showers about seven-thirtyish," Chandler checked his watch. "They go twelve hour shifts, seven to seven. This way when they come in they get lost in rush hour traffic, no tails."

Hoyt headed down to the locker room and passed a couple of patrol cops leaving after a long night's work. He heard the shower running when he came through the door and patiently waited until it finally ceased.

"You new around here?"

"Nah, I'm from Manhattan. I heard you were working undercover in Brighton. I'm with the Nightcrawler Squad, we've been poking around. Just wanted to be sure we weren't stepping on any toes over there."

"You'll never see our toes, my friend."

Robert Sciaraffo stood 5'9", weighed 210 pounds on a husky frame that had been hardened by routine weightlifting. There was no doubt that he was capable of leading the hijack team. Only there was something else that Hoyt saw in the muscular build, draped only by a towel. This man could have been on a SWAT team, maybe even with the Navy SEALs. He could have done anything Sabrina could have…maybe better.

Something told Hoyt that this was the one.

This was the Nightcrawler.

# Chapter Seven

The two black Ford Explorers rumbled along the road near the Jacqueline Kennedy Onassis Reservoir at Central Park at 2 AM that morning. Although it was decommissioned as a public reservoir in 1993 due to pollution concerns, it still fed the Pool and the Harlem Meer and was a popular place for residents and tourists alike. The terrorists decided that by releasing a liquid form of the hybrid Ebola strain into the water, all who contacted the virus would carry the plague directly into midtown Manhattan and trigger a new epidemic.

The Explorers were each occupied by three men. In the rear were packed five metal tanks apiece which were filled with the Ebola contaminant. As they slowed to a halt near the 85th Street fenceline, two men emerged from the vehicle before signaling the coast was clear. Their confederates exited the vehicle and walked about the grassy knoll before continuing their mission. Five of the men were Nigerians from Boko Haram. Their leader was the monster Apollyon.

"Make haste!" Apollyon ordered, gesturing toward the fenceline. "Let us proceed!"

One of the blacks produced a high-tech laser gun that was still in a developmental stage with Russian military researchers. One of the prototypes had been stolen by Chechen agents and brought back to Dagestan. It was shipped to New York and placed in the hands of Tryzub. The Boko Haram commando activated the device and waited a minute for its transistors to power up. At length, it was fully powered so that the agent was able to fire the laser beam at the steel fence. The terrorists watched in awe as the laser cut through the steel like butter, making a hole big enough for even the seven-foot Apollyon to access.

They next pulled the tanks from the SUVs. Each Nigerian took two tanks with them as they slipped through the fence and made their way towards the lake. They came within yards of the shoreline and rested their burdens as Apollyon determined their next course of action.

"Say, you fellows are breaking quite a few city ordinances here," an electronically-distorted voice called from the shadows beneath a nearby tree. "Destroying public property, trespassing…if I was you I'd leave before the cops show up."

"The Nightcrawler!" Apollyon thundered. "Impossible! How could anyone have known we were here! Kill him!"

The Nigerians whipped out their Uzis holstered on their belts, firing at the shadowy figure as it dove into the reservoir. They rushed to the water and poured automatic rounds at the spot where the vigilante disappeared. Within a minute they had exhausted their clips and were forced to reload.

"Fools!" Apollyon trudged over to where an electronic device sat amidst the dark weeds. "It is a trick! This man is not in the water!"

He reached down and pulled up a sophisticated hologram projector that depicted the Nightcrawler and transmitted a recorded voice. He threw it against the tree in a rage, and as if on cue, the vigilante popped out from behind it. The Nightcrawler darted past Apollyon and fired a powdery spray at the Nigerians, who dropped as vermin upon contact. The vigilante turned towards Apollyon, who knocked the gun flying across the grass before dropping his assailant with a murderous right cross.

"Your gas gun will be of no further use to you," Apollyon snarled as the Nightcrawler tried to regain a solid footing. "You will beg for your life before I beat you to death!"

With that, the Nightcrawler sprang from a crouch and swung a killing blow to Apollyon's head. The vigilante had titanium bars embedded in the forearm guards of the black uniform which managed to dent Apollyon's metal helmet. The indentation forced a salient into Apollyon's brow that caused him great distraction. He responded by cocking and firing the harpoon-like devices affixed to his own metallic gloves, which drove three metal spikes from each fist into the Nightcrawler's chest.

Once again it was another scientific breakthrough that turned the tide of battle. The vigilante had been experimenting with graphene, using the two-dimensional carbon honeycomb material as a surface coating for combat gear. It was found to be ten times more effective than steel in dissipating kinetic energy, and Apollyon's darts proved to be no exception. The Chechen assassin charged his victim and was astonished as the Nightcrawler threw a right roundhouse kick that smashed into the dented helmet. Apollyon hissed with pain as he staggered back, the vigilante pouncing into a defensive stance.

"Look how much bigger you are than me, and you still fight dirty," the Nightcrawler taunted him. "You better get your friends and scram before something worse happens to you."

"I'll cut your eyes out and feed them to my dogs!" Apollyon roared, activating yet another device in his oversized metallic gloves. Like the vigilante, he also had sheaths embedded along the outer forearms of his combat suit. Only these allowed foot-long bayonet-like blades to project from beneath the ridges of Apollyon's fists. He rushed the Nightcrawler, who managed to dodge a vicious backhanded slash. A second thrust embedded a blade nearly two inches into the trunk of the nearby tree.

"Ha, ha, you missed," the Nightcrawler mocked him as the sound of emergency vehicles echoed in the distance. "This is your last chance. You better get those clowns outta here before the cops show up."

Apollyon swore blasphemous oaths as he gathered the choking Boko Haram agents, guiding them towards the aperture cut into the fence. As an afterthought, he drew the laser gun and pointed it at the Nightcrawler, who ducked safely behind the tree.

"This is far from over!" Apollyon roared as he shoved the Nigerians into their vehicles. "Our next meeting will be our last, I swear by Hell!"

"I sure hope so," the Nightcrawler baited him. "You should wash that uniform the next time, it kinda stinks."

As it turned out, the emergency vehicles were fire trucks en route to an alarm event. The vigilante watched the black SUVs drive off before producing a small hand-held amplifier.

"All bums!" the Nightcrawler called into the bushes along the fenceline. "Come out and earn a good wage! Help protect our city against terrorists! I will pay all bums who help me wrap these tanks!"

Slowly the foliage began rustling as sleeping vagrants were roused from their places of refuge. They had dug tunnels beneath the fenceline and set up cardboard boxes hidden from plain sight. These were their temporary domiciles, and they lived from day to day not knowing what their future held. The offer of a couple of bucks was irresistible, and they mustered themselves to see what the dark figure had in mind.

The vigilante had prepared the field according to information provided by Max Mironov. As a result, the homeless people stepped up and were given rolls of plastic wrapping. They next stacked the tanks together according to instructions and wrapped them until their rolls were spent. They then returned the cardboard spools in exchange for a fifty-dollar bill. In less than a half hour, the unfortunates were singing the praises of the Nightcrawler as police cars headed directly to the scene.

Within minutes, the scene was deserted save for the plastic-wrapped bundle of canisters. The police searched high and low but the hobos and the Nightcrawler were nowhere to be found.

* * *

"You know, the only thing I can think of that's worse than driving to a funeral on Christmas morning on a Sunday is driving to New fricking Jersey."

"Hey, I asked you over the phone not to come if you didn't want to."

"Yeah, well, who would've held your hand out here otherwise?"

"You guys get me confused," Jerry Loverdi called from the back seat. "Which one of you guys are the senior officer here?"

"Who gets the Egg Mc Muffin? We're near the bottom of the bag."

"I'll take it if no one else wants it."

"See, that's my whole point. You take any damn thing if no one else'll take it."

"Piss off, Bob, for cripes' sake, why don't you turn on the radio?"

Hoyt Wexford shook his head as he saw Bob Methot alongside him turning his head, trying to hide his silent chuckling. He saw Jerry and Don Conroy munching on their Steak Mc Muffins and was glad that at least someone could endure the trip in good spirits.

He was roused from his sleep at sunrise by Lieutenant Shreve, who reported that a fourth member of the Brighton Five had turned themselves in. Max Mironov had called the unpublished number on the business card given to him by Lori Murphy. He came across as cocksure and full of bluster, but experienced cops knew that he was approaching his breaking point. They drove him out to the safe house in Newark where plainclothes cops were guarding him until the Nightcrawler Squad arrived.

"So what're you gonna tell us, wise guy?" Bob Methot swaggered into Max's cheap motel room along the outskirts of South Newark. He was followed by Hoyt, who took a seat in a worn armchair by the window. He steepled his fingers, staring at Max who sat on the double bed against the wall. He wore a black T-shirt along with the black suit pants and $200 shoes he had on when he was brought here.

"What do you wanna hear?"

"Your friends swear up and down you've been snitching for the Nightcrawler. Word on the street has it that the Grozny brothers think you gave up one of their colleagues in an attempted terror attack. Our people think that's why you called."

"That's three different questions. What do you think, you're gonna confuse me so I contradict myself? Maybe I just sit here and listen to you. You got some pretty good stories."

"Look, Cossack, I stop paying the tab on this room and you're a dead man. Any gangbanger on the street makes a call to Brighton and they'll bring you back there in a car trunk."

"You put my friends up and you turn me loose? Why do I doubt that?"

"Your friend Lori gave up the Crawler. I need you to corroborate her statement."

"Do *what*?" Max squinted.

"C'mon, Russkie. Describe him to me. How big is he?"

"He's about six-foot-nine, three hundred pounds, just like it says in the Internet."

"Hey, asshole, get the hell outta here," Bob threw open the door so that it slammed against the wall. "Now."

"C'mon, Bob, close the door," Hoyt said quietly. "Look, who do you think you're talking to? Lori has him at five-nine, two-ten. What does he do, inflate himself before he comes to see you?"

"She only seen him one time. We got attacked by the Brighton hijackers and the Crawler was watching my back. He didn't get close enough for Lori to size him up. She saw him at a distance, maybe she figured he was a lot smaller."

"So tell me about Tammy Chekhov."

"Tell you what?" Max got up and went around the bed to the nightstand for a cigarette.

"Gimme one, topknot," Bob came over and snatched one away from Max.

"You know all the insults," Max smirked. "You must be big with the ladies."

"Yeah, your mother thinks I'm pretty hot," Bob turned his back to Max.

"What did you say?"

"We'll ask the questions," Hoyt interceded. "Lori told us you knew Tammy. Carissa backed her up."

"You're a damned cop," Max flared. "You know Tammy was murdered a few months ago."

"We also know his brother got whacked by the Mob," Bob took on a conciliatory tone. "They whacked him out because they thought he was snitching to the Crawler. It's the same reason why they whacked Tammy. It's why we think they're looking for you."

"The Crawler got to Tammy's brother because a girl he loved died shooting China White," Max's face darkened. "Back then the Crawler was hitting on drug dealers. Tammy's brother hated them for getting her hooked. The Crawler compromised him somehow and he agreed to snitch. It wasn't the Mafiya, it was Tryzub. There was a Mob war going on, and Tammy's brother was a convenient target."

"So what, the Crawler approached Tammy after his brother got whacked?"

"What do you think?" Max blew Marlboro smoke at Bob. "He lost his connection, he went for the next best thing. Tammy was sick over his brother's death. He wanted revenge, but what could he do? You show a gun to the Mafiya, they show guns to your family. He agreed with the Nightcrawler, but somehow the Mafiya figured it out."

"And so you got involved."

"This is what you Westerners can never figure out," Max stressed. "In Russia, it's blood for blood. Tammy was my friend. They beat him to death. I visited him in the hospital, I would have never recognized him. A friend is like a brother from a different mother. I could not live with myself if I stood by and did nothing. The Nightcrawler preys on people like us. He senses weakness, he pries us loose from the pack. He doesn't care. When Tammy was killed, he sought me out. After I'm killed, he'll find another."

"So what kind of deal did he make with you?" Hoyt was terse, catching Bob off-guard. "Was it all about revenge? He said he'd take down Tryzub if you cooperated?"

"You people really need to do your homework," Max shook his head. "If you need a tutor I'm sure we can come to a financial arrangement."

"Listen, borscht breath, you got no leverage here," Bob got in his face. "You get us up to speed right here, right now, or I drive you downtown and let the Lipkis know where I dropped you off."

"Yeah, right," Max rolled his eyes.

"C'mon, Max," Hoyt cajoled. "Our snitches told us the Russkies and the Chechens kissed and made up. They won't admit it because they don't want Homeland Security standing on their crotches. They're keeping us a half chapter behind in their storyline. We know Apollyon has the Mafiya's full support. That's why Lipki wants you dead for tipping the Crawler off on the JKO Reservoir attack."

"Let me ask you something," Max stared at Hoyt. "Do you think Lipki announced to us that Apollyon was going to dump the plague into the reservoir? Do you think that we were given maps and invitations, or there was some sort of Internet event for us to attend?"

"Someone gave Apollyon up. That's the reality of it. All indications point to you. It sure as hell wasn't the Groznys."

"Okay," Max relented. "Look, the Nightcrawler is doing ten times as much for this City—for its people—than you pigs are. That's a fact."

"Watch your mouth, punk," Bob stepped forth menacingly.

"Go ahead, punch my lights out, I don't care," Max was vehement. "You cops, you and the police in Russia, in Dagestan, you're all the same. You do your jobs, you take your assignments, you follow procedure, you do everything you are told to do and then some, then you go home at the end of the day. The Nightcrawler doesn't do a job, he doesn't get paid. Maybe he's a sick sonofabitch on some crazy mission, but he does what he thinks is right. He doesn't go home. He's always out there. He's saved my life, and he will avenge those who helped him do the right thing. He's not like you, he's better than you. When you go home is when the Nightcrawler goes to work."

"What does he sound like?" Hoyt demanded. "He must have some distinguishing characteristics. We need to find this man. Stop jacking us around."

"I think he has throat cancer," Max mellowed out somewhat. "He speaks through one of those voiceboxes. I—and that's just me—I think he may be like one of those feminine men. There's just certain things about him. You know, the body language. He crosses his legs funny, sits forward funny. You know my friend Chuck, sometimes he's like him."

"So you think the Nightcrawler's gay?" Hoyt challenged him.

"Yeah," Max exhaled. "Maybe."

"So we're looking for a six-nine, three-hundred pound fag?" Bob grunted.

"I don't think this guy's giving us everything he knows," Hoyt pounced from his seat. "The Crawler's smaller than what you say he is. Admit it."

"Gotta watch for coaching, kid," Bob muttered under his breath.

"I don't know who Lori thought she saw, but the man you're looking for is a 300-pound *goluboy*. This is who he is, this is who you want. You bring him here, and I will identify him for you. I am fairly sure I am the only one who has seen him. Bring him, and I will condemn him."

Hoyt felt his guts churning as they left the hotel room, nodding to the plain-clothes cops outside the room on the second floor balcony. They trotted down the metal steps to where Jerry and Don awaited. The three of them slipped into Hoyt's Camry and headed towards the Newark Bay Bridge. They stopped at a gas station for a four-pack of Guinness, then cruised towards the bridge and parked beneath it on a landing near the river.

"This stuff's like water," Bob took a sip from his can before producing his flask from his inside jacket pocket.

"It's more than enough for me at this time of day," Hoyt held out his hand as Bob offered him a taste of cognac.

"Hell no," Jerry chuckled, stepping away from Bob's flask. "I gotta go back to Brighton. Those Russkies think I'm drunk, they're liable to take their chances. They hate my guts as it is."

"You got that right," Don laughed, turning away from Bob. "I never heard the word Irish used along with so many cuss words in my life. I almost feel like I'm working Flatbush."

"We're running the meter on this deal, guys," Bob leveled with them "What do we got?"

"I'm squeezing the crap out of the Groznys," Jerry exhaled. "I got their dealers running for cover. Only they've gone to a wartime economy. They're biting the bullet, and street crime's skyrocketing. The addicts are going crazy trying to buy a fix. We got home invasions left and right, druggies breaking into anyplace they think they can score. Chan's bringing all kinds of heat down on me, and I'm getting calls from Shreve every other day."

"Shreve's calling you?" Hoyt squinted. "Why didn't you tell me?"

"What am I gonna do, rat the Lieutenant? I'm just telling you guys, I'm catching serious flak and I'm not getting anything for it."

"Neither am I," Don admitted. "I've got guys all over the street looking for the Yakovs' next card game. Nobody's playing. The only whores out selling are the junkie skanks. There's rumors they moved their business across the Bridge to Manhattan, but I got no proof. I'd bet my ass that if I go over after them, they'll bring it right back here. They're a step ahead of me, and it's their neighborhood. This isn't gonna happen before the end of the year, guys. No way."

"Here's to morale boosting," Hoyt said sarcastically, pouring down his Guinness. The others spent little time chugging cans, and within the hour they dropped Jerry and Don off at Police Plaza.

Hoyt drove down to Chinatown, where Bob had taken to parking his car to avoid Mafiya snitches spotting his vehicle near the Plaza. Hoyt stood by Bob as Methot lit a Camel, sitting on the fender of his Lexus.

"They're closing us down, kid," Bob exhaled a stream of smoke. "Two, maybe three weeks. You know the whole thing was about giving you a chance to finger the Crawler and take the heat off your old lady."

"Who told you that?" Hoyt narrowed his eyes.

"Hey, who hooked you up with Vosberg? I've been around the block and back a few times. Guys like Vosberg don't exactly post their business cards on bulletin boards."

"I know who you are and what you are, Bob," Hoyt said tersely. "We whacked out that bank robber in broad daylight a few weeks ago and they acted like we parked in a handicapped space. I appreciate whatever you've done—what you are doing for me. I won't forget it."

"They found your girl dressed like the Crawler about an hour after that Russian chick got killed at her office complex," Bob was emphatic. "The Boko Haram team got killed by a grenade, and she survived. People think she made a deal with the Crawler and it backfired. That Nightcrawler's a cold-blooded son of a bitch, kid. He's left a trail of bodies behind him. The Chekhov brothers, the Octagon, who knows who else. Sabrina was just collateral damage to this guy. If Lipki catches up to Mironov and his crew, the Crawler won't even blink."

"So why would anyone think Sabrina would deal with the Nightcrawler?"

"Everyone knows she gave up her dream of joining the force when her father died. Put two and two together. That punk Kelly Stone from HS isn't just looking at Sabrina because of Boko Haram. There's a question about that gas the Crawler uses. That stuff he was using against the Octagon was bona fide chemical weaponry, world-class. He's been downgrading the quality over the past year, but how and for what? Lots of people think it points to Sabrina, especially after that train wreck at the BCC. The only thing that's gonna get Stone off her case is a new Crawler suspect. Captain Willard threw you a big bone, kid, but he's gonna take it back if you can't hold onto it."

"You know I've met the Nightcrawler more than a couple of times. Bob Sciaraffo fits the bill. There's no way in hell the man's six-foot-nine. Sciaraffo's a war vet, in awesome physical condition, probably running that Brighton hijacker team…how in hell can it not be him?"

"What are you gonna go? Go to Chandler? Shreve? Willard? Chief Madden? You're gonna denounce a war hero and a decorated cop? With what? If you can't back it up, your career is over. The whole force'll turn its back on you. Think long and hard about what you're doing."

"I need help," Hoyt stared into Bob's eyes. "All I got is you and Jerry and Donnie. If we can't get it done as a team, I'll never make it alone. Sabrina can't defend herself. If the press gets hold of this, it'll ruin BCC. She'll lose everything. If she ever wakes up, what'll she wake up to?"

"Hey, I'm on your side," Bob patted his shoulder. "Just remember, sometimes you can develop such a strong suspicion that it becomes a fixation. It happens to every cop at one time or another. You start forcing the round peg into the square hole, no matter what it takes. But it works both ways. It doesn't *have* to be Sciaraffo. You understand what I'm saying?"

"Yeah," Hoyt stared across the street at the Chinese people milling across Canal Street from them, going about their business. "Yeah. I hear you."

"Good," Bob put on his sunglasses and walked around to the driver's side of the silvery car. "We'll find us a Nightcrawler. It'll be okay."

"Yeah," Hoyt managed a smile. "We'll work it out."

\* \* \*

Rita Hunt had devoted most of her personal time to the Force of God Christian Church on the Bowery over the past couple of years. She had survived a tempestuous relationship back in Warren County in her home state of Kentucky, and relocated to NYC to pick up the pieces. One of the ministers of the Church had persuaded her to visit, and once she heard Pastor Matt speak, she was there to stay. She was cautious of getting involved in another relationship and grew standoffish around men who expressed interest in her. She confided in the Pastor, who encouraged her to remain vigilant until she was sure she found the right one.

Kelly Stone was one of the most handsome men she had met, but his self-assuredness seemed to border on cockiness at times. She accepted an offer to go for coffee after visiting Sabrina at the hospital and running into him. She convinced herself she was doing it for Sabrina, trying to find out why he had such an interest in her comatose friend. Only Kelly's charm was disarming, and she soon agreed to have dinner with him that weekend. It was one of the best times she had in a long time, only she was turned off when he tried to give her a French kiss at the end of the night. She would not return his calls thereafter, and finally he gave up.

It was a different story with Dzhokhar Zhivago. The Assistant Secretary to the Foreign Minister of Dagestan sent her an invitation to a cocktail party at the embassy a week ago. She had soft drinks all evening but was enchanted by the debonair Chechen and the glamorous ambiance of the grand parlor. He, unlike Kelly, ended the evening by kissing her hand and expressing hope they would get together again soon. She thought about him quite a bit since then, and his offer to accompany him to a reception at the Waldorf-Astoria Hotel was gladly accepted.

She bought a new outfit for the occasion, a knee-length cerulean silk dress with dark blue nylons, heels and purse that appeared as ebon from a distance. She looked gorgeous and was told so by Dzhokhar, who treated her as royalty in escorting her from his limousine to the entrance of the fabled hotel. He asked her to wait for him in the lounge area as he registered at the desk for the private event. She waited patiently, though curious that there did not seem to be anyone else arriving for what she perceived as a gala event.

"Come, my dear. The Ambassador has reserved a penthouse suite for the gathering," he entreated her. "It seems that a number of guests were delayed at the airport, so we may have to await their arrival. I have been assured that the caviar and champagne will be right behind us."

"My, my," she smiled. "It does sound like quite a deal."

They took the elevator to the Cole Porter Suite, the magnificent quarters affording them a sweeping view of the Manhattan skyline. She marveled at the crystal chandeliers hanging above the regally-furnished room, thanking Dzhokhar for a soft drink as he accessed the well-stocked portable bar. He kept the door wide open, explaining that the other guests would arrive shortly.

He sat across from her on an overstuffed velvet armchair, telling her an amusing anecdote about his first assignment at the Embassy. Only he was interrupted by a call that he claimed was from the Ambassador, and excused himself as he walked over to the enormous sliding glass patio door to converse in Russian.

All of a sudden she began feeling drowsy, and when she tried to stand up to shake it off she found her legs to be entirely uncooperative. She turned to look at Dzhokhar, who put away his cell phone and smiled knowingly at her.

"A thousand pardons, my dear," he said softly. "It seems the Rohypnol is taking its effect. It takes about fifteen minutes to manifest itself, and about six hours to wear off. By then we will be well on our way along our adventure together."

"You…you drugged me? You brought me here to rape me?" she was astonished.

"Nothing quite so unscrupulous, though I admit it is a stimulating thought. Actually, I intend to hold you hostage until the friend of your friend makes themselves known. I am fairly certain that Sabrina Brooks has a strong connection with the vigilante Nightcrawler. I believe that if he finds out that you have been abducted because of him, he will make himself known in order to make a deal."

"You've got to be out of your mind!" Rita exclaimed. "I don't know anything about the Nightcrawler. Neither does Bree. She got kidnapped by those looney tune Boko Haram nut jobs and was rescued by the Nightcrawler, but that doesn't make them friends. He doesn't know me from Betty Boop. He's not gonna make a deal with you for me even if you put up an ad on TV."

"We shall see, won't we? I already notified my associates that I had you where we wanted you. In a short while you will be nearly incoherent, and I'll have a couple of men take you down to the service area and escort you out of the building. In less than an hour you will be on your way to the waterfront where you will be held off-shore until the Nightcrawler reaches out to us."

"You won't get away with this!" she tried to get up but her muscles were rapidly losing energy. "The people at the Church are gonna know I've gone missing. They'll call the police, and soon the FBI will get involved. I was seeing an agent from Homeland Security. You can bet your butt that he'll be looking for you and your whole rotten gang!"

"Unfortunately, Homeland Security has been looking for my comrades and me for quite some time. As you can see, they have been both inefficient and unsuccessful. I'm quite certain that there will be an initial furor over your disappearance, but that will only cause the Nightcrawler to join the fray. That will be precisely what we are anticipating."

"Why wait? We can cut to the chase right here."

They were startled at the sound of the glass door sliding open, followed by the electronically distorted voice. Their hearts leapt in their chests at the sight of the vigilante standing at the threshold.

"The Nightcrawler!" they chorused.

"You know, I'd bet my bottom dollar I know who you are. Even though you don't look so big without that dumb-looking costume of yours. I already beat your butt twice already, so why don't you just give it up before you get hurt?"

"You little worm!" Dzhokhar raged, charging to the bar and grabbing a liquor bottle. He smashed it against the rail and rushed his adversary with a vengeance. Only the dark figure drew the gas gun from its holster and fired, dousing the giant with a white powder. Rita stared in awe as Dzhokhar dropped to the ground, gagging and choking as his eyes, nose and mouth were clogged with mucus.

"You really ought to be more careful about who you date," the Nightcrawler chided her. "Especially a good-looking girl like you."

"You… you saved my life," she staggered to her feet as the dusky shape rushed to steady her. Rita's knees suddenly buckled, and she fell into her rescuer's arms.

"Whoa there. You'll be okay. I'll call the front desk and have them send the police and an ambulance. You be sure and press charges, don't let this dirt bag back on the streets. Diplomatic immunity or not, when they find the Rohypnol in your system they'll send him to Rikers Island. He won't talk his way out of this one."

"You're my hero," she gushed drunkenly. "I love you."

"Yeah, I love you too, but I gotta go," the Nightcrawler weakly tried to pull loose. At once Rita pressed her lips against the Nightcrawler's mouthpiece.

"Hey, hey. I'm not that easy, y'know," the vigilante lowered her gently back to the couch, stepping away and glancing over at the choking Dzhokhar. "Just kidding. I gotta go. I'll call the desk, just sit tight."

Rita watched as the Nightcrawler disappeared from the patio. She dropped back into a dreamy state, oblivious of the giant crawling around the carpet behind her until the police were swarming the suite.

* * *

Ron Simmonds told his friends he was not up to going out for beers under the watchful eyes of their undercover guardians that evening at a local tavern. He had a headache and an upset stomach and felt like he needed to sleep it off. He woke up in the middle of the night and had to go to the bathroom a couple of times due to diarrhea and vomiting. By morning he was burning with fever and was taken to the hospital by a couple of officers. That afternoon he was diagnosed with Ebola and would not return to the motel. The Brighton Four, now the Brighton Three, were relocated to another motel just outside the nearby city of Harrison.

* * *

Rita Hunt stayed overnight at Bellevue Hospital, a couple of floors from where Bree Brooks was kept. Her modest Obamacare policy covered the visit, and she left the next morning at eight AM. She had gotten calls from both Hoyt Wexford and Kelly Stone. Both of them mentioned one another and requested that they meet with her for a brief interview. She was not looking forward to meeting Kelly just now but saw no way to refuse. They suggested a meet at a coffee house not far from the Church on the Bowery and she obliged them.

She was dressed in a thin leather jacket, a t-shirt and jeans with her hair tied back in a ponytail. Regardless, she was easily the most beautiful woman in the restaurant. Her face was somewhat drawn from her recent experience and she did not feel very comfortable meeting with these two on such short notice. They both hugged her lightly as they met her outside. They entered together and took a table in the rear where they were beyond earshot of the other patrons.

It was a difficult situation for all concerned. Rita knew that Kelly must have been jealous over her avoiding him while accepting a date with Dzhokhar. He still had a duty to perform, and she knew that it was bothering Hoyt that Kelly was still snooping around Bree and her friends. Most likely he felt that Kelly was using Rita to get to Bree. Even worse, Hoyt was heading a Nightcrawler Squad that was searching for an unknown suspect while the trail was pointing back to his fiancée.

"I hate to be going by-the-book with you," Hoyt emphasized after they re-iterated their concern for her health and wellbeing. "It's just that we're both fighting against time here. You said in your statement that the Nightcrawler accused Zhivago of being Apollyon."

"Yes he did," Rita stirred Splenda into her cappuccino. "He said that he was easy to recognize even without the costume. Dzhokhar never once denied it. Besides, the threats he made against me made it easy to believe he was with those Chechen terrorists. I think it was Tryzub, that gang that hired Boko Haram to kidnap Bree…and kill Dariya."

Rita knew it was difficult for both men with their own feelings for her. She paused to daub a tear from her eye with her napkin as she thought of Dariya Romanova.

"I…I'm sorry, guys. I just haven't gotten over Dariya's passing yet. Bree and Dariya were my best friends."

"It's been hard for all of us," Hoyt nodded.

"We're playing tug-of-war over Zhivago as we speak," Kelly revealed. "My people want him transported to Leavenworth before we make arrangements to get him to Guantanamo Bay. The NYPD and the State of New York wants him sent to Rikers Island so they can subpoena the Chechen Mob and the Mafiya on a RICO charge. Meanwhile the Dagestanis are filing a writ of habeas corpus so they can make a deal based on diplomatic immunity."

"Do you mean to tell me they're trying to let him go free? After trying to kidnap me?" she exploded.

"That's what the Dagestanis have in mind. I doubt very much my superiors will let this one loose. If we can prove he's Apollyon, it may be enough to shut the entire Tryzub gang down once and for all. You start threatening to send people to Gitmo, they'll tell you the color of their mother's underwear."

"Now, honestly, Kelly, I have asked you time and again not to make off-color remarks in my presence," Rita blushed.

"I'm sorry, hon," he reached over and patted her wrist. She could feel the resentment in Hoyt's gaze as he observed the fleeting contact. "I apologize."

"Well, okay," she drawled softly, finding the soft spot in their hearts.

"I wouldn't put a whole lot of faith in that move to Gitmo," Hoyt replied. "Your commander-in-chief's catching a lot of flak for not closing it down. I think things'll move along a lot smoother if you help us get him to Rikers and take him down on a RICO."

"So you two are fighting amongst yourselves while his people are fixing to set him free," she flared.

"We talked this over before we came up here," Hoyt admitted. "They're gonna need you to testify against Zhivago. If you agree to do it, we're gonna have to place you under protective custody."

"You mean you're gonna arrest me?" Rita asked in disbelief.

"That's not how it works," Kelly assured her. "You get to stay in an out-of-state hotel room. You can go shopping and carry on as normal. Only you'd be under police guard and asked to stay away from crowded public places."

"Well, what about my job?"

"You'll be compensated. Plus you work for Pastor Matt," Hoyt pointed out. "I'm sure he'd have no problem with this."

"You don't sound like I have much of a choice."

"Doll, the situation got out of hand when that Russian creep set his sights on you," Kelly insisted. "It's not your fault. He just used you as a way to get to Sabrina."

"I sure know how to pick 'em, huh?" her eyes were sad. "He is a good-looking man, with all those connections, and the way he carried himself. How the heck could anyone know? When I think of him being that psychopath on that video on TV, that Apollyon...and to think he was mixed up with those dirty dogs who killed Dariya...I am so ashamed of myself."

"We all make mistakes," Kelly said gently. "The main thing is that we have our friends by our side to help us get back on our feet."

"He's right," Hoyt agreed. "Plus it's obvious that Zhivago is a powerful man with major connections. We have to get you somewhere safe, that's the most important thing right now."

"So do I even get to go home and pack?"

"It may not be a good idea. I'll make some calls, arrange to have whatever you want picked up at Neiman Marcus or wherever," Kelly replied.

"Neiman Marcus? Not on the NYPD's budget."

"You can pick up the hotel tab. We'll handle the rest."

"My, my. Listen to 'em fighting over little old me."

"So how big was he, the Nightcrawler?" Hoyt leaned towards her from across the table. "Was he as big as Zhivago? We've got Zhivago at six-nine, over two seventy-five."

"Yeah, he is a big boy," Rita nodded. "I wore my tallest heels when we went out."

"You went out with him before?" Kelly's eyes were pained.

"That is my business, sir," she said pointedly.

"Nightcrawler, Ree. How big?" Hoyt was insistent.

"Well, geez, Hoyt. I told your buddies that I was stoned out of my head. I am not a drinking woman by any means, but I do declare that I had never been that drunk in my life. I can't tell you with all certainty that I remember anything, but I do remember portions like it was in a dream. Now, I did get up to give the Nightcrawler a thank-you kiss…"

"Damn, Rita, is there anyone you didn't kiss up there?" Kelly was irked.

"Excuse me?" she flushed.

"Okay, you got up to kiss him. How big was he?" Hoyt pressed.

"I don't know, I kinda fell up against his chest, so I guess he was about a foot taller than me."

"Dammit," Hoyt exhaled. He knew Rita was about as tall as Bree, which would have made the Nightcrawler well over six feet tall. It was pushing Robert Sciaraffo off his list.

"Okay, look, we should really start making things happen here," Kelly decided. "I'll have a couple of cars over here in a few minutes and we'll get Rita to a safe house outside of the City."

"Not happening. I'm bringing her with me to Harrison."

"Do you really think a squad of plainclothes cops can protect her better than the Federal government?"

"I'm not going anywhere with you, Mr. Smarty Pants. You've got a smart mouth and you need to learn to mind your manners."

"Rita, I—"

"Come on," Rita rose to her feet, gathering her purse. "Let's go."

"I'll give you a call," Hoyt said before escorting her out of the coffeehouse.

Kelly sat and stared at the door long after they left, wondering what it would take to get back in that long-legged Kentucky woman's good graces again.

* * *

The Prayer For Peace Rally in East Harlem was as sand in the eyes of State and Federal administrations. Homeland Security officials were scrambling desperately to persuade lawmakers to declare Boko Haram a terror organization. Conservative strategists pushed back, insistent that upgrading Boko Haram's status would afford them prestige beyond that of just another militant gang. HS insisted that ISIS' recognition of the group had already given them that distinction, but the politicians would not budge.

Mayor John Jordan next declared that the scheduled parade would pose a threat to the health of the residents of Harlem, considering the Ebola plague that was still afflicting the metropolitan area. He also warned that the event would severely compromise the NYPD's resources, in light of the fact that they had lost twenty percent of their force to the plague. Plus, the City's budget was nearly depleted due to the emergency funding of health programs. Yet the rally organizers would not relent, insisting they had a Constitutional right to a peaceful gathering.

Donna Summer knew that the rally would provide a foolproof cover for moving the million-dollar shipment of China White. Her soldiers had transported the goods from the meeting place with Apollyon to the Boko Haram Mosque a few days ago. Now they had to move it to a distribution point where her captains could pick it up for delivery to their street teams. Only she knew the authorities were watching the mosque with an eagle eye. She would have to act very carefully lest all their plans be destroyed.

Only a few hundred people turned out for the parade that began at the mosque on 137th Street and ended on Lenox Avenue and 110th Street. Most wore paper breath masks and plastic gloves out of concern for the plague. Alternately, members of the 137th Street Gang wore black kerchiefs over their noses and mouths. They, like those of Boko Haram, also wore black khalats that made them easily identifiable. Once again the NYPD units were placed in check by the tactic as this new gang paraphernalia was being considered as religious apparel until further notice. Thus the gang was able to display their colors without fear of harassment or interdiction.

Media sources would note that there seemed to be as many law enforcement officers as civilians at the parade as the NYPD came out in force. From horseback units to riot squads, the police maintained a high profile as the participants chanted and pranced for the cameras. They carried Islamic State banners, Boko Haram flags and Malcolm X posters in proclaiming their activist agenda and right to free speech. Peace seemed to be the least of their objectives, though symbols of doves and olive branches could be seen on a couple of placards.

The crowds responded with the rallying cry of all those who had been galvanized by the Ferguson riots in Missouri 2014. They waved signs reading 'BLACK LIVES MATTER' and 'HANDS UP DON'T SHOOT', chanting anti-police slogans and 'Allah Akbar'. The police chafed under the provocations, realizing that this was turning into a propaganda victory for Boko Haram. They remained stoic as the revelers laughed and mocked them, taking full advantage of the occasion in venting their frustration on the City administration.

Donna and Philemon Rubidium had planned the demonstration to take place on a Friday morning, which encouraged many students to ditch school throughout the area. As the morning progressed, more and more kids were cutting classes in order to attend. It seemed as if there were as many teens on the street as there were on the local campuses by noontime. The event began taking on a carnival atmosphere, but as the rally ended things began taking on a darker turn.

Boko Haram had constructed a specially-made hearse wagon bearing a coffin that was inscribed as containing a dead Bill of Rights. Each of the ten amendments of the Constitution were posted on the coffin, which was festooned with red, white and blue decorations alongside funeral wreaths. Muslim women in burkas wailed over the coffin, creating an imposing theatrical scenario. Only law enforcement officials had no way of knowing that the wagon was rigged with a false bottom. It would allow the drug traffickers to bring the China White packages from the mosque onto the hearse at parade's end.

"Sister Donna, I do not see how making this poison available to our people is fulfilling the will of Allah," Philemon stressed as the Boko Haram agents brought the metal suitcases from the basement safe up to the doorway of the mosque. "This narcotic destroys lives, it breeds crime and corrupts our communities. Surely nothing good can come of this other than blood money."

"This is not going to our people, how many times must I tell you?" she blazed. "Muslims do not use drugs. This is meant for the infidels, the fake Christians who swear by Jesus yet work for corporations who steal from our people. They take drugs to block their consciences. We sell them drugs to speed them along the road to Hell. The only reason drugs are illegal is to prevent the corporations from being corrupted. We will afflict them with a cancer that they will never cut out."

"How can this be the way of the Koran?" he was adamant.

"This is jihad. This is a holy war against the infidels. As it is written, if you are not on the side of Allah you stand against him. The ways of the unbeliever and the disobedient lead to death."

Philemon watched in astonishment as events progressed. As the parade ended, the floats and flatbeds began returning towards the mosque where they were dismantled. Homeland Security and the NYPD were already watching the building, but were distracted by activity on the street as unruly students began disrupting traffic. The street units tried to disperse the mob, but as if on cue, the teens began running down the streets towards the residential buildings.

As they were chased by the police, they swarmed into the tenements as a flock of birds. The cops stood by uncertainly, unsure as to which of the students actually lived there. It gave the kids time to regroup and begin racing down the streets again. The officers were in pursuit, and the teens began bottlenecking en route to the mosque on 137th Street. The horseback units began forming skirmish lines along Lenox Avenue, though the students avoided them in joining the cluster around the mosque.

It was impossible for the surveillance units to see that the metal suitcases had been passed out the door of the mosque into the waiting hands of Boko Haram agents. They moved them along to their teammates until it reached the hands of those stationed by the casket. They slipped the cases into the top coffin, draped so that no one could see the levers shifting to rotate the box beneath the wagon bed. With that, the Boko Haram agents took the top coffin from the hearse as the seemingly empty wagon rolled away.

Minutes later, the agents allowed the students to open the coffin, revealing it empty in broad daylight. The hearse containing the hidden casket with the suitcases disappeared from sight.

\* \* \*

Carissa Fermanagh had received numerous texts from her family over the past couple of weeks. They were concerned for her safety and pressed her for details on her protective custody situation. She reluctantly adhered to Hoyt Wexford's admonition that no information should be transmitted electronically under any condition. Only it was a series of texts between her and her cousin Margaret that had finally broken her resolve.

Margaret lived on Long Island, having moved from Brooklyn where she spent her high school years hanging out with Carissa. They had smoked lots of pot together before Margaret moved on and Carissa began dealing dope with Max and the gang. They kept in touch though they grew distant over the years. It was recently that Margaret indicated she felt as if she was being watched by strangers. She wasn't sure why and didn't know where to turn.

At first it was people driving by her home and parking out front after dark. She then felt as if cars or people were following her on the street. Next she had friends mentioning that strangers were approaching them, asking if they knew her. Over the past week, the stalkers were making no attempts to hide themselves as they stared at her across city streets in broad daylight. She wanted to confront them but was too afraid. She thought of calling the police but her marijuana habit could get her into trouble with the ramped-up drug laws.

She asked Carissa if there was a possibility she could rent a room near where she was staying and hide out there for a while. Carissa was hesitant and discouraging at first, but the messages grew more insistent bordering on hysteria. When her cousin began pleading that she feared for her life, Carissa felt she had little choice. She eventually broke down and made plans to meet Margaret near the motel in Harrison at midnight.

What she had no way of knowing was that Tryzub had located Margaret and coerced her into making contact. They, in turn, subcontracted the Lipki Gang into abducting Carissa. It would be a simple matter to force Carissa to divulge the whereabouts of Max and the others in Harrison. From there they would be able to use explosives in killing the snitches and ending the threat. The job was assigned to the Yakov brothers, who brought two of their own assassins along with them.

The kidnappers cruised off Route 1 South and circled around to the deserted parking lot of the Post Road Inn. They spotted the blue 2000 Ford Contour parked at a distance from the large, well-lit sign out front as agreed. They drove past the vehicle as if preparing to leave the premises, then slowed to a halt before one of the killers exited their 2015 Lincoln and headed towards the car. He drew his pistol as he approached, the Lincoln idling as it lowered its windows.

The abductor crept towards the driver's side, peering at the red-haired figure he was certain to be Carissa. He pointed his gun at her head, heedless of whether she spotted him in her rearview mirrors. Only she did not budge, and he took a circular approach as he stepped in front of the open window. He was perplexed at the veil of hair draped over her face, and suddenly the situation dawned on him as his gaze was met by a pair of glassy eyes.

"Holy cow!" he yelled back at his comrades before unleashing a stream of blasphemous oaths in his native Russian. "The bitch is dead!"

"The hell you say!" Vitali Yakov led the others as they vaulted from the Lincoln. "Pull her out of there, she's playing possum!"

"Hold on, you fools!" Timur cried out. "It's not the Irishwoman. It's Deadwoman!"

At once there was a loud rustling in the tree under which the Contour was parked. A dark shape caused a frightening impact on the roof of the Ford. The first gunman was hit with a kick in the face which smashed his front teeth into his mouth. The boot of the figure was reinforced with a substance that was yet relatively unknown to all mankind.

Before Sabrina Brooks' accident, the BCC had secretly been experimenting with a high-entropy alloy that had a higher strength-to-weight ratio than any metal in existence. It was a combination of lithium, magnesium, titanium, aluminum and scandium, creating a nanocrystalline alloy of low density but unparalleled strength. It was comparable to aluminum, but far stronger than titanium. Its impact on bone was as a hammer against glass.

The dark avenger drew its gas gun, hurling it like a tomahawk at Timur Yakov. It hit him between the eyes, dropping him like a fallen ox.

"Now we've got you," Vitali snarled. "You fool, you threw your gun away."

"You think I need a gun to beat you two?" the Nightcrawler laughed, jumping off the Contour and confronting the remaining gunman. The Russian went for his shoulder holster as the vigilante kicked him with full force in the shin. The bone broke like a rotted board, causing excruciating pain to shoot as a lightning bolt into the killer's brain. He fell to the pavement, crying like a baby in an agony he had never felt in his lifetime.

"You little bastard!" Vitali tackled the vigilante. He stood six foot and weighed two hundred pounds, considerably bigger than the shadowy figure. Only the Nightcrawler grabbed the lapels of his $500 silk suit, twisting and hurling the Russian in a hip toss to the asphalt. The fight ended as the avenger drove a fist into Yakov's jaw, breaking it like a pretzel.

"Hey!" a morbidly obese security guard came waddling from the main office across the lot in their direction. "What the heck's going on over there?"

"You'd better call an ambulance, these fellows are in a bad way," the Nightcrawler called out to him.

"You stop right there!" the fat man screamed. "I arrest you!"

"Move over, I'm driving," the Nightcrawler opened the driver's door and shoved Deadwoman aside. The dark knight then hopped into the Contour and sped off into the night.

# Chapter Eight

Sabrina Brooks dreamed of a time when she and Jon Aeppli first began realizing the possibilities in their breakthroughs while testing the limits of indentation. They developed a technique by which they measured both yield strength and ultimate tensile strength. They built a machine with a cylindrical flat diamond that could be driven into a test specimen at a controlled loading rate. Such a technique allowing for direct correlation of macro tensile properties was relatively unheard of. It gave them unprecedented YS/UTS mapping with which they could detect crucial defects on their prototypical designs.

"If only your father had lived to see the advancements we've witnessed over just these past couple of years," Jon shook his head. "Science is just developing by leaps and bounds. We never dreamed of some of the things that are being accomplished. I'm only thankful that it was his daughter that I was able to see these things happen with."

"And it's not just test-tube mixing and matching we're doing," Sabrina insisted. "The things we're doing will benefit lots of people. We're gonna do a whole lot of good. We are gonna save lives, I promise you."

"That's where it starts getting complicated," Jon shook his head, taking a seat on one of the high stools in the restricted lab area at the BCC complex. "We may be able to do something with the graphene, but the scandium we need for the nanocrystalline hybrid is way too expensive. The Company doesn't have the money to float that boat. Plus, that takes us back to Square One."

"Jon, we've got the government contracts. We came within weeks of discovering a cure for the AIDS virus. If we get the Ebola contract, we'll be able to redirect all that research and make it happen. We can do this, the money is there," Sabrina insisted.

"I'm talking about you going out there and risking your life, Bree," Jon stared at her. "The right thing would be for us to develop these materials and sell them to the government for use by law enforcement. The wrong thing is you using this technology and taking your life in your own hands."

"We've already discussed this time and again," she grew upset. "You see how Hoyt's getting compromised and hamstrung by the system. Look at all the good the Nightcrawler's done. Can you imagine all the things that could've happened if there was no Nightcrawler? How can you just give up and walk away from all this? Look, I know I can't do this forever. Why can't we just see things through to where there's an acceptable crime rate out there? No more terrorist threats, no more crisis situations. Don't you think we can make that happen?"

"Maybe not in this world. Maybe not in this day and age. This is the 21$^{st}$ century, kid. There never was an Islamic State, no global terrorist organization. They didn't have gangs like Tryzub, like Boko Haram, these militant gangs wanting to destroy society over some twisted religious prerogatives. They never had entire communities rising up against their own police forces, fighting against the very agencies that are sworn to protect and defend them. This is a crazy world we live in. How can you seriously believe one person – one woman – can make a difference?"

"We have to try, Jon. Don't you think we got to try?"

"I think of you like a daughter, Bree. The daughter I never had," Jon's voice grew husky. "You ask me to sacrifice too much. You ask me to sacrifice my best friend's daughter. You ask me to sacrifice my daughter. You ask for too much. Far too much."

Hoyt Wexford saw her body twitch and leaped up to hover over her. Shakeera Smith had been watching by the door and rushed in as Hoyt bounded from his seat. She saw the grief in his eyes as he realized it was a momentary spasm, and stood helpless as he imploded before her. He sank into his chair at her bedside, holding her hand softly against his face as he wept disconsolately.

"If only there was something – anything – I could do," the nurse came behind him and touched his shoulder. "Seeing the two of you like this breaks my heart."

"Oh, my gosh, if she would just wake up, just please wake up," he sobbed, kissing her alabaster hands and her carefully painted scarlet nails.

"Is that the way she did them?" Shakeera asked softly. "Is her makeup okay? I had those pictures you gave me, and I tries to make her just like she used to be."

"Yes," he managed. "She looks very beautiful. Thank you."

"You know they is taking her for tests today."

"I know. Her friends are coming, we're going to pray for her in the chapel together."

"Is you a religious man, Detective Wexford?"

"Why, I…" he paused, caught off-guard by the question. "Well, I…maybe not so much before. Bree was a churchgoer, and I…well…yeah, I guess so. I need to be, you know."

"Thass good. I believe in a higher spiritual power too. This life too hard to make it without it. If there ain't no God, I don't know what's what no more."

Hoyt numbly made it to the elevator and rode down to the lobby, waiting patiently until the others arrived.

"Hello."

"It's Jon," the voice responded on his cell phone.

"How's it going?"

"I won't be able to make it today. My son is having a birthday party for his wife. I hate like hell not to be there with you. I hope you understand."

"I do. I know Bree would."

There was a pause.

"Hoyt, you know I'd do anything…"

"Hey, Jon, I know. She'd be very upset if she knew you weren't there with your family. She's always looked at you like a father, and I see you in that light as well. Not to worry, okay?"

He saw Pastor Matt Mitchell arriving, but his face darkened at the sight of Rita being accompanied by Kelly Stone. The Pastor shook hands with him and he exchanged hugs with Rita. He beckoned Kelly to one side as the other two entered the chapel together.

"Hey, I appreciate you bringing Rita here, but it wasn't necessary. I think the Nightcrawler pretty well closed down the Harrison option for Tryzub."

"It wasn't a problem. I was glad to do it."

"Look, I don't want to be a dick here, but I don't think you should be here. It's not who you are, it's who you represent. I think it'd be obscene."

"I thought you and I had an understanding. I told you I was the only one here on HS business, and I would make sure it stayed like that. You can't turn it on and off like that. You insult me to put me on the other side of the fence like this."

"You don't even know her."

"I feel like I do. Besides, she's Rita's best friend. And I'm here with Rita."

"All right," Hoyt relented. "C'mon, then."

They entered the chapel together, joining Rita Hunt as Pastor Matt Mitchell led them in prayer for the recovery of Sabrina Brooks.

\* \* \*

The personnel department at Police Plaza was notified that both Jerry Loverdi and Don Conroy had been admitted to Bellevue Hospital the next morning. They left Brooklyn the night before feeling under the weather. By dawn their conditions had worsened so that they visited emergency clinics in their respective neighborhoods. Both were sent directly to Bellevue via ambulance and admitted as Ebola victims. Everyone connected to Loverdi and Conroy realized that their illnesses would effectively seal the fate of the Nightcrawler Squad.

\* \* \*

"Can you beat this crap? Of all the rotten luck."

"I'm just worried about Jerry and Don. They're alright fellas. It's a damn shame that they've come into this."

Hoyt Wexford and Bob Methot met at Cody's American Bar and Grill on Court and Amity Street in Brooklyn that afternoon after learning of their fellow officers' plight. Hoyt was not much of a drinker but had no problem joining Bob for beers on this morning. He knew that the Nightcrawler Squad was finished, but was more distraught over the fate of two men he had come to regard as friends.

"Did you ever hear the story about how they earned their gold badges?"

"No, not really."

"They were working undercover with the Vice Squad at the 76th Precinct in Brooklyn," Bob thanked the bartender for a bowl of complimentary chips. "They had this low-level dealer working as a snitch inside the Phantom Outlaws in the Gowanus Projects. This punk was a real loser, the kind of guy who would get real messed up and start running his mouth at the wrong place and time. Turns out he was at a rave at some banger's house and started bragging about all his connections. Unfortunately he mentioned a couple of guys who were already on the radar for being police informers. The Outlaws put the word out, and one of their top lieutenants found out he was making the rounds at the Gowanus Projects one afternoon."

"Broad daylight, huh?" Hoyt smiled wryly, dipping a chip into a small dish of hot sauce. He noticed the bartender was scanning an Off-Track Betting form at the end of the bar, undoubtedly listening to every word. He had no doubt this fellow was one of Bob's biggest fans.

"Yep. The banger came out with six of his top goons and braced the snitch right in the middle of the walkway over there between Hoyt and Bond Street. Kids were just getting out of school, people were hanging out the windows, everybody saw what was happening. The banger walked up and jammed a gun underneath the snitch's chin, giving him the badmouth before the sendoff. Well, Jerry and Donny knew what was gonna go down. They made their way through the crowd and drew their guns. Jerry stuck his gun under the banger's chin, and Donny jammed his into the snitch's neck. Nobody knew what to do, maybe two, three hundred people watching from all over the projects. Right there in broad daylight, middle of the afternoon."

"Talk about a hard situation," Hoyt chuckled, shaking his head.

"You bet your ass," Bob took a swig of beer. "There were lots of bangers showing guns, talking trash, but none of them drew on Jerry and Donny. They had a crowd around them ten men deep, and it was like a swarm moving step by step, like a procession. This ring of bangers made its way out to Hoyt Street where the squad cars were waiting. The cops moved in and hauled them all off to the paddy wagon. The bangers never did figure out who Jerry and Donny were planning to take out. After they got their detective shields, they got transferred to Narcotics in Manhattan. They were there until they got the call to come in with us."

"Luck of the draw," Hoyt raised his glass.

"Whole damn career's the luck of the draw. From your first day out of the academy to the day you cash your first retirement check – or go six feet under – it's the luck of the draw."

"Amen," said Hoyt.

"Hey, guys," the bartender got off his stool, retrieving the remote control to the widescreen TV behind the bar. "You might wanna see this."

"Good morning, this is Amber Tant for Eyewitness News with exclusive coverage of an event taking place at the Dagestan Embassy in midtown Manhattan," the auburn-haired newscaster stood in front of the building as her cameraman focused their equipment on the front gate. "The mysterious group known as the Brighton Hijackers have been revealed to be part of a sting operation being conducted by the Brooklyn NYPD. Less than an hour ago, they arrived here at the embassy with Homeland Security agents. They entered the building and served warrants for the arrest of Ilya Stastny, the Director of the Russian-Chechen Relations Bureau in Dagestan. Stastny has been accused of conspiring with the Chechen based Tryzub terror group to smuggle two million dollars' worth of China White heroin into the US. A vehicle registered to Stastny was confiscated at a New York warehouse with the heroin welded into the chassis. The so-called Brighton Hijackers received a tip from an informant which resulted in Stastny's arrest."

"Can you believe it?" Hoyt stared at the plasma TV screen.

"Here we have footage of the Brighton Hijackers bringing Stastny out of the building into a waiting truck," Amber had her crew put up a video on the screen. "He was transported to the Metropolitan Correctional Center in downtown Manhattan where he was formally charged with drug trafficking. The leader of the undercover team has been identified as Detective Robert Sciaraffo, a ten-year veteran of the force and a decorated war veteran having served in Iraq and Afghanistan."

"That pretty well takes him off our Nightcrawler list," Bob shook his head, watching Sciaraffo as he smiled and waved at the cameras. "We can't touch him with a ten-foot pole after this."

The realization hit Hoyt like a ton of bricks. It was like a steel door being slammed in his face. If the Nightcrawler copycat had been working with the Hijackers, he would never be able to find out now. Robert Sciaraffo would probably be invited to the White House after this. But if Bree had set something like this up in the event she was incapacitated, why had she not told him or Jon? Did she think he would run the bogus Nightcrawler to the ground to exonerate her? Most likely. She planned it through, and all roads that led to Sciaraffo were cut off.

"Cheer up, kid, at least we won't be sent over to work under Chandler in some kind of Mafiya task force," Bob noted. "I'll bet the big boys in Moscow'll be wanting Lipki's head on a pike after this. With Max Mironov having turned, the Yakovs under arrest along with Zhivago, and now this, I'm sure they're figuring it's time for a change."

"Dammit, Bob, where do you think they're putting them all?" realization suddenly dawned on Hoyt. "You don't suppose they're all going to the MCC? All Tryzub would need to do is stage some kind of attack and give them all a shot at busting out."

"Geez, kid, you got a point," Bob swiveled off his barstool and headed for the restroom with his cell phone. "Lemme make a couple of calls."

The notion made him break a cold sweat. After having attempted assaults on the Wall Street area and the Jackie O Reservoir, making a move on the MCC would be child's play for Tryzub. Even with the suspected Apollyon on ice, how could anyone question the possibility that there was yet another homicidal maniac out there who would risk his life to spring his comrades? Although their apostle Donna Summer denied it, Boko Haram was part of the Islamic State, and they could make a move at any moment. They had the entire 137$^{th}$ Street Gang at their disposal, which added over one hundred hardcore gangbangers to their core strength. Making it worse was the pride and arrogance of Chief Madden and Captain Willard. They would gladly be blown up inside the MCC itself before admitting that it could be overwhelmed by a street gang.

"Hey, kid, not to worry," Bob practically skipped out of the restroom after a few minutes. "Great news."

"What's that?" Hoyt was almost as wide-eyed as the bartender, who could not help but gaze expectantly at Bob.

"Looks like HQ's thinking the same way we are for once," Bob smiled. "Dzhokhar Zhivago's getting shipped off to Rikers."

\* \* \*

At three that afternoon, two Sheriff's Department squad cars idled their engines as a team of SWAT riflemen escorted a handcuffed Dzhokhar Zhivago into an armored personnel truck. There were four decorated veterans in each squad car, a total of twelve heavily-armed, seasoned fighters guarding the man everyone suspected of being the supervillain Apollyon. Driving him from the MCC to the waterfront where a Coast Guard gunship awaited was a relatively short run, but they were warned there could be hazards along the way.

Lieutenant Bob Lacey was both confident and somewhat unconcerned. He was an Iraq veteran, a twenty-year man who had seen lots of action on the force. He would end his career with SWAT, hoping to earn perhaps one last accreditation before it was over. He almost hoped that the Russkie's pals would try to spring him loose. Maybe Bob Sciaraffo was the man of the hour, but if the Reds hit this transport, Lacey would be the man of the year.

"Here he comes," Steve Jensen, a black cop who was also a war vet on the road to retirement, nodded to the six armed officers escorting their prisoner from the lower level ramp up to the loading dock. "That's a big honky."

Although the armed escort averaged six feet tall, the four men came even with Zhivago's shoulders in height. The prisoner was clad in a bright orange jumpsuit, his wrists and ankles hobbled by chains, but it seemed as if he might break his shackles at any moment. Both Lacey and Jensen marveled at the sight of one of the biggest men either of them had ever seen.

"If that Nightcrawler took this guy out three times like they say," Lacey shook his head, "I'd sure as hell never want to go head to head against *that* son of a bitch."

"All them Russians we nailed swear that the Crawler has titanium knuckles in his gloves," Jensen smirked. "I sure would like to pick me up a pair."

What bothered Lacey most was the demeanor exhibited by Zhivago from the time he emerged from the complex. He had a swagger unlike anyone about to be transported to Rikers Island en route to Guantanamo Bay. His eyes were as cameras searching the area, taking full note of his surroundings, as if analyzing the situation in preparing his own move. Lacey had no doubt that the man would seize any opportunity to chance an escape. Only under such a guard as this the man had to realize his life would surely be forfeit.

Lacey's plan seemed foolproof, considering that they would be moving in pre-lunch hour traffic through downtown Manhattan. A lead car carrying four riflemen would be followed by the armored car, tailed in turn by a second car holding four more SWAT officers. Jensen would be in the passenger seat of the lead car, Lacey riding shotgun in the third car. A helicopter carrying a sniper tandem was ready to launch from the rooftop of the Police Plaza complex upon call. If the Chechens made a move on the convoy, they would have to pry Zhivago from the armored car after neutralizing two teams of operatives at both ends of the truck. Not to mention dealing with the chopper that had an ETA[1] of less than five minutes.

---

1. estimated time of arrival

Tryzub's gambit consisted of two cars wedging the convoy in front and behind, with two motorcycles bracketing the unmarked cars on either side. The bikers would paralyze the escorts, trapping the armored car between the immobilized cars. It gave the intercept team less than five minutes to free Zhivago from the armored car before the attack helicopter and ground reinforcements arrived.

Had the discipline of the escort team been less rigorous, any of the police officers would have seen the breaking news surrounding the Zhivago arrest and remanding to Rikers. Independent news sources discovered that Dzhokhar Zhivago was an alias being used by Cesaro Francium. The Chechen was a former member of the KGB who defected to Tryzub and was a key figure in numerous terror attacks by the militant organization. The Russian government was demanding the extradition of Francium, who they suspected of being the mysterious Apollyon. The US State Department objected, claiming that Francium's connections were such that he would never arrive in Moscow to see a day of trial or imprisonment.

Most NYPD tacticians and analysts concurred that Lacey's confidence in his team was such that news of Zhivago's true identity would not have swayed him. Neither would the fact that the 137th Street Gang had been largely reorganized as the result of Boko Haram guerillas joining their ranks. The fighters coming over from Nigeria had killed dozens of men apiece and were highly skilled in terror strategy and military tactics. The gangsters gave place to the militants, four of whom were riding choppers and dispatched to eliminate the motorized guard escorting Apollyon to the landing zone along the New York harbor.

"Hey, Steve, I'm picking up vehicles moving high-speed towards your six," Lacey radioed Jensen as he studied his GPS scanner. "They're coming in parallel, looks like motorbikes."

"We're on it," Jensen replied. "My boys are locked and loaded. Big Dude, you copy?"

"Got it covered," the leader of the team inside the armored car assured them. "Got three guards surrounding the prisoner in triangle formation. He's not going anywhere but dockside."

"What in hell—?" were the last words heard from the lips of Steve Jensen. The biker on the passenger side drew up alongside the squad car so that his gunman could fire a blast from a sawed-off shotgun through the window into

Jensen's face. The driver caught glass shards in his eyes, blinding him as he fought desperately to maintain control of the vehicle.

Lacey was entirely caught off-guard by what happened next. The second Boko Haram cyclist drew alongside the driver's side, his passenger firing a double blast at the officer behind the wheel. Though mortally wounded, the officer managed to slam on the brakes as a vehicle sailed through the intersection and squealed to a halt before them. The armored car barely avoided a collision with the lead car as the driver nearly swerved before stopping.

"Get out of the car! Take up positions!" Lacey ordered, wiping blood clots and pieces of glass from his face. "Archangel One, this is Delivery Man! We're under attack, need backup now!"

Inside the truck, the guards were perplexed as Apollyon dropped into a fetal position, covering his head. At once there was a deafening explosion as the Boko Haram guerillas tossed a grenade beneath the rear door of the truck. The metal was ripped asunder, the roar depriving the guards of their hearing as their eardrums were perforated. They were staggered and unable to respond as the agents tossed items into the truck to Apollyon.

The officers watched helplessly as Apollyon pulled on his helmet, cape, chest protector, gloves and boots. The giant wasted little effort in breaking the necks of the three men before reaching into the driver's compartment and crushing the back of the man's skull with a titanium-coated fist.

"Come on, brother!" a Nigerian yelled. "There is little time to lose!"

Although the helicopter responded within three minutes, the Tryzub team had accomplished their task in two minutes. Gunmen from the intercept vehicles had murdered the escort team with shotgun fire, and Apollyon had dragged Bob Lacey from his hiding place after the SWAT leader was mortally wounded.

"I will let you live to deliver my message," Apollyon hauled Lacey from the pavement by the front of his flak jacket. "I will unleash the final plague from the skies above New York City, and no one will escape my vengeance. The people of this city have incurred my wrath, and one hundred million dollars is all that can save them."

With that, the intercept vehicles streaked off into downtown traffic as the NYPD helicopter descended on the scene of carnage left behind.

\* \* \*

Max Mironov painfully spat a glob of blood onto the concrete floor upon which his chair was bolted. He was clad only in his boxer shorts, his wrists bound behind the back of the seat and his ankles fastened to its front legs. His face was covered with bruises and he could barely see through his swollen eyes. He tried to focus on the four gangsters standing in the shadows beyond the glaring overhead light, smirking back at him.

At once he heard the door unlock as a figure stepped into the room. He noticed how the demeanor of his captors changed, and he knew at once it was Stanislav Lipki.

"My young friend, I hoped we would meet again under far more pleasant circumstances," Lipki strode past the gangsters, past where Max was bound in remaining just beyond the lamplight. "Ever since your visit to my home, I've heard nothing of you but disturbing rumors. Your absence made me believe the rumors were true. Now, all of a sudden, here you are at risk of your very life. I came here to hear your confession from your own lips."

"You'd better start talking, you little rat," Pyotr Grozny stepped forth and threw a crushing right cross at Max's jaw.

"Why would I..." Max gurgled.

"Why?" Nestor Grozny began walking towards Max. "Here's why."

"Why would I come back here if I was guilty?" he gasped, staring at Lipki. "You think I didn't hear the rumors? After the Nightcrawler stopped Apollyon at Central Park, everyone said I ratted him out. It couldn't have been the Yakovs or the Groznys, or Yuri Kurskov. They've been around too long, No, it must have been the new guy, don't you know. Let's blame it on him and everything'll be fine. Once he and his friends are gone, all will return to normal. Only it didn't work that way, did it?"

"What do you mean?" Lipki held a restraining finger toward Nestor.

"What did the Yakovs have to gain by capturing Carissa? Did they really think it would cause me to give myself up? Then all of a sudden, once they're taken into custody, the Brighton Hijackers turn in their cards and Ilya Stastny is taken down. When is that last time you heard from the Yakovs? Perhaps they made a different choice than I. I came back here and risked my life to prove my loyalty. Maybe it is they who took the one-way trip to Wyoming."

"You little scumbag," Yuri came over and grabbed him by the throat. "I've known Timur and Vitali all my life. I'll make you eat your words before I kill you."

"Of course you will. If they believe the Yakovs are snitches, why would they think you knew nothing? Suspicion is like a cancer, it eats everything and everyone alive. It divides us. Once I'm gone, it'll be just you and the Groznys. Who will be next?"

"Hold on," Lipki walked over, causing Yuri to step away. "Who offered you a trip to Wyoming?"

"Homeland Security," Max managed, a long stream of bloody drool hanging from his lip. "A man called Kelly Stone. He's the one sent from Washington to catch the Nightcrawler. They were using the NYPD's Nightcrawler Squad as their bloodhounds. They were working independently of the Brighton Hijackers. Hoyt Wexford picked me up and made it looked like I squealed. My friends came in and he took us to Jersey. When the Yakovs came for Carissa, Kelly took over. He cut me loose and told me he'd put out the word that I ratted you out. He said that now he had the Yakovs, he didn't need me."

"This is a pack of lies! The Yakovs would never roll!" Yuri hissed.

"The Manhattan DA's putting together a RICO conspiracy charge against the Brooklyn Mafiya," Max revealed. "The Feds're threatening to send anyone connected to Tryzub to Guantanamo Bay. Either way, you're looking at twenty to thirty-year stretches. Show me a man who wouldn't think of rolling from beneath that weight."

"And of course, you did not roll," Lipki smiled tautly.

"My life is here in Brighton. All my family, all my friends. I thought I had a future in your crew until now. What would my life be in Wyoming, or the Dakotas, or wherever? They might as well toss me in Leavenworth, or Guantanamo, or wherever. If I cannot come back here, I might as well be dead."

"I've checked his rags and his wallet, nothing," Pyotr dumped Max's rolled bundle of clothes on the floor beside him. "He's not wearing a wire, to be sure."

None of them would have suspected that the Nightcrawler had sewn a tiny microchip into the seam of Max's underwear. It was sophisticated enough to pick up all sound within a twenty-foot radius. Anyone who searched the garment would have mistaken it for a wad of cloth.

"We will keep him here until the day and time comes to put the last phase of the operation into effect," Lipki announced. "You will bring him with you, and we will see whether or not he is the cause of the leak. If he is, then the Nightcrawler will watch him take his last breath. If he is not, then he shall be given his share of the bounty and restored into our fellowship."

"Mr. Lipki…" Yuri blurted.

"Yes?" Lipki stared at him.

"Your will be done, my *bugor*," Yuri relented.

The four men watched as the ruthless gang leader disappeared into the shadows.

\* \* \*

Apollyon had delivered a final warning to the Mayor's Office the next day, including the number of a Swiss bank account on the encrypted CD. He assured the City administration that, if the $100 million demand was not paid, his Ebola weapon would be detonated in a public place that would cause the infestation of a highly populated area. The Mayor contacted Homeland Security immediately, who in turn updated Kelly Stone.

"Boris Semenko? Who in hell is Boris Semenko?"

"He's a Colonel in the Federal Security Service," Kelly revealed to Hoyt Wexford as the men met beneath the Brooklyn Bridge later that afternoon. "The Russians got in touch with the State Department last night, requesting that Semenko be released. He went by the alias of Ilya Stastny while acting as the Director of the Russian-Chechen Relations Bureau in Dagestan. They say they want to return Semenko to Moscow to face charges of corruption."

"Are they insane? If he's in with Tryzub, he'll be hooking up with Apollyon in carrying out that terror attack."

"They won't let him go during the terror alert, but if or when it passes, he'll probably walk," Kelly shook his head. "Our only hope is taking Apollyon down. And I hate to say it, but a lot of it will depend on the Nightcrawler getting involved."

"So is that why you called me here? You think there's something I'm not telling you?"

"Look, I kept up my end of the bargain. I pulled all our people out of Bellevue. All I've got is a secretary calling once a week to see how Sabrina's coming along. You gave me Robert Sciaraffo's name, and now I've got a round-the-clock team watching him on vacation in the Bahamas. You can't tell me all your team could come up with was Sciaraffo."

"Hey, you've got the entire Government at your back, and all you could do was stakeout Bree's hospital room. The Nightcrawler's damn near invisible.

The Mafiya can't stop him, Tryzub can't take him out, and he practically blew the cover off the Brighton Hijackers. If you caught the Nightcrawler you'd probably catch Apollyon, but you're nowhere close. Yet you come down here and ask me how come I haven't done it yet."

"I've got Damien Blakey up my butt. He reports directly to Sandra Flores, the Deputy Director. She is responsible to Marlon Ritz, the Director himself. That maniac Apollyon is threatening to unleash the mother of all plagues on this City in twenty-four hours. I'm grasping for straws here, Hoyt. Anything you got can save lives."

"All right," Hoyt relented. "I've got a lead, a slim lead. Bob and I are going to check it out. If you get a call from me in the next twenty-four hours, you come running. Got it?"

"That's all you're gonna tell me?" Kelly's eyes narrowed. "I can take you and Bob in for obstructing."

"Then the lead goes up in smoke. Bob's tougher than I am, and I'm never gonna give you jack. You should know that."

"All right. This better work. I tell you this: if this City gets hit with that chemical weapon, and I find out there's anything that could have prevented it, you'll get hung out to dry for it."

"It'll be the least of my worries."

The two men went their separate ways, Hoyt walking down the cobblestone streets in the opposite direction as Kelly drove towards Cadman Plaza en route to the Manhattan Bridge.

"So are we set?" Bob Methot asked as Hoyt returned to his Lexus.

"Yep," Hoyt replied. "All we have to do now is wait until the Nightcrawler makes his move."

* * *

The heroin shipment intercepted in Boris Semenko's vehicle left Tryzub's remaining fortune in the hands of Chakra Khan. The woman known as Donna Summer gave Philemon Rubidium notice that her million-dollar supply of China White had to be moved immediately. Police pressure in the East Harlem area had proved unbearable. Homeland Security had used the Ebola plague as a subterfuge to set up mobile treatment centers throughout Harlem which served as surveillance units. The word in the 'hood was that the medical trucks were wiping both Ebola and the 137th Street Gang off the streets.

Philemon found himself in an untenable situation. His ministry to the Muslim community had suffered irreparable damage as a result of Chakra's Boko Haram gambit. Most devout Muslims distanced themselves from the mosque and denounced the Boko Haram movement entirely. The murders of the 137th Street Gang members who dissented created a great rift within the East Harlem neighborhood. Their families cried out for justice and laid blame at the door of the 137th Street Mosque and the feet of Philemon Rubidium.

Chakra sent four of her most trusted Boko Haram gunmen to Philemon's home that evening. Unknown to him, their Ford Explorer contained the million-dollar cases of China White. They were on the way to Four Seasons Hotel on East 57th Street where Chakra Khan and four Tryzub agents awaited to move the heroin to hideouts throughout the Tri-State area.

Philemon was sick to his stomach as he and his escorts rode the elevator to their luxury penthouse suite, carrying the aluminum suitcases in plain sight. The gunmen carried on as if nothing was amiss, chewing gum and prattling on in their native Nigerian. Philemon did his best to keep his knees from shaking. He imagined that everyone in the lobby was an undercover narcotics agent ready to take them all into custody. He knew that if they were captured with such a huge load of heroin, they would go to jail for the rest of their lives.

Yet Chakra had prepared this move exceedingly well. She had presented Philemon as the face of the organization though it was she who did most of the public speaking. He was front and center at their meetings with the NAACP, and all their publicity focused on Philemon as a prominent community leader and Muslim minister. It made him virtually untouchable, and a move against him without probable cause would have proven disastrous to the law enforcement agencies monitoring East Harlem.

"Greetings, my friends, it is so good to see you," Chakra was resplendent in a gold tiara and a crimson silk gown. Her spiked heels caused her to tower over a foot higher than her male comrades. "This will be an enormous source of income to our organization once the seed is planted. Yet it will be but a trickle compared to the river of gold that will flow to us once Apollyon's demand is met."

"I do not believe the Americans would pay such a price," a Chechen said as he opened the suitcases seated upon the large glass table in the middle of the huge white-carpeted parlor. "What guarantee would they have that Apollyon would not detonate the canister anyway? This product that we have here is more precious than gold. This is what we have to look forward to."

"I, for one, do not want to be anywhere near this island when Apollyon unleashes the plague," his fellow Chechen replied. "Millions of people will die. I will far more comfortable starting a drug epidemic in New Jersey."

"It would be a real shame, it's such a beautiful city," an electronically-distorted voice called from the enormous patio area. "You should come out here to appreciate the view."

The occupants of the room felt a thrill run down their spines. The characteristic trait of the vigilante was well known. The Chechens drew their guns and charged, but were met with a great cloud of white gas. They fell to the rug as poisoned insects before a mighty crash ensued with a shower of broken glass spraying the room.

"It is the Nightcrawler!" Chakra screamed. "Kill him!"

"How could he have known where we are? There must be—*unggh*!" one of the Nigerians gasped as the emptied gas gun crushed his orbital socket. The Nightcrawler next hurtled through the air, slamming into two Nigerians and knocking them backwards over a large sofa. The fourth black man rushed towards the skirmish, only to have his liver ruptured by a kick from a titanium-armored boot. His comrades regained their feet before their jaws were broken by a flurry of punches and kicks.

"Stop!" Chakra commanded. "This is a religious meeting! You have no right!"

At once the Nightcrawler grabbed a plastic-wrapped kilo of heroin and bashed it over Chakra's head. It was torn open by the points on the tiara, causing the powder to cascade in an avalanche over Chakra's hair and shoulders.

"Ha, ha, look at you," the vigilante taunted as Chakra tried to wipe the powder from her face. She could not help but inhale the narcotic and was nearly paralyzed within seconds.

"The police," Philemon croaked dazedly as they could hear hammering at the suite entrance.

"You did the right thing by cooperating," the Nightcrawler patted his shoulder before heading back out to the patio. "I let my police contacts know what you did, your name'll be cleared. They'll take Boko Haram down and let you put your ministry back together. I may not believe in what you're praying, but I'll sure as heck fight for your right to pray it."

"Bless you, my friend," Philemon managed, looking at the bodies strewn about him. "You are a good man."

"Yeah?" the Nightcrawler chuckled before departing. "We'll see about that."

The police broke into the room, arresting the occupants and wondering how the Nightcrawler could have vanished from a terrace over twenty stories above the streets of New York.

# Chapter Nine

"Make no mistake," Mayor John Jordan spoke at a press conference the next morning that was being broadcast across the planet. "Despite the exhilarating success of the Brooks Chemical Company, we are in no way minimizing the threat imposed by the Tryzub terror gang and Cesaro Francium, the man known as Apollyon. Our researchers have confirmed the existence of a mutated Ebola virus retrieved from the chemical weapons captured by the NYPD. We have not determined whether the BCC antidote will prove effective against the mutant strain. Therefore, we will maintain a high-level security alert throughout the City and urge our community to exercise utmost caution over the next twenty-four hours. We urge all citizens to avoid public places as much as possible and report any suspicious activity to the authorities. The biggest manhunt in our City's history is currently underway. We have the full cooperation of the Muslim community, the Russian-American community and the Chechen-American community in standing shoulder-to-shoulder with their fellow New Yorkers against these fanatics."

The arrest of the woman known as Donna Summer became second page news in wake of the deadline imposed by Tryzub on New York City. Exposed as Nigerian militant Chakra Khan, the Boko Haram advocate was charged with possession of narcotics and held without bail. The Chechens and the Nigerians swore that the Nightcrawler had brought the heroin to the suite to frame them, but lobby cameras caught the Boko Haram gunmen bringing the aluminum suitcases into the hotel. They were also charged with the possession of illegal military-grade weapons. Once again, descriptions of the vigilante were conflicting. Chakra Khan claimed that the Nightcrawler was under six foot tall. Philemon Rubidium asserted he was seven foot tall and bulletproof.

"Since the terror threat was issued by Tryzub, world leaders from around the globe have contacted City Hall and expressed their support in our efforts to defeat these extremists. We have the full cooperation of the Federal Government and Homeland Security, and we will not rest until these madmen are brought to justice. The global community stands behind us in our pledge to put these criminals away once and for all. We know that our international society will never be safe until these conspirators are prosecuted and convicted, never to see the light of day for the rest of their natural lives."

The Russian government, seizing the opportunity to distract the world press from the political turmoil in Eastern Europe, targeted Boris Semenko as a major Tryzub terror chieftain. The Russian President declared that Semenko should be charged with treason, a crime punishable by death if convicted. The Russian newspaper *Pravda* emphasized that Tryzub was an international criminal organization with no viable connections to either Chechnya or Dagestan. Neither was there any established proof that Tryzub was working in collusion with the Russian Mafiya. It, like the Islamic State, was a rogue enterprise preying on the civilized nations of the world. Boris Semenko eventually was released into the custody of the Russian Security Service, never to be seen again.

New Yorkers were filled with exultation as replays of the newscasts from City Hall were interrupted by a special report. Amber Tant on Good Morning America reported live on the scene of a police action in Lower Manhattan, where major news broadcasters soon converged to deliver yet another story to be heard around the world.

"The New York City Police Department has reported the seizure of a truck filled with explosives en route to an undisclosed destination here in Manhattan," the lovely correspondent announced. "Officers on the scene have announced that the truck contained one thousand pounds of volatile material, an amount equal to that used in the Oklahoma City Bombing of 1995. The suspects are described as four men in their twenties appearing to be Chechen nationals. Authorities are investigating the suspects to determine any possible ties to the Chechen-based Tryzub terror group. The police were tipped off by a female informer by phone, who may or may not have ties to the mysterious Nightcrawler. The vigilante has been the subject of a police search for over a year and is wanted for questioning in over a dozen high-profile criminal cases. Although the Nightcrawler is credited for apprehending several criminal suspects over that period, the information available to the vigilante has been deemed by authorities as being of a 'highly suspicious nature'."

Shakeera Smith was among those glued in place before the TV set, fascinated how things were developing so rapidly. It was beginning to resemble her own microcosm, where she had observed her vigil at Sabrina Brooks' bedside day after day. All of a sudden she had been given new marching orders, and she had no idea when she was going to come down or where she was going to land.

"Don't pay no nevermind to all that big talk, child," Minnie Ratched startled her, the hefty woman appeared behind her as if out of nowhere. "They're out there doing deals with the devil, I guarantee you that. As soon as they arrest one they find out they have ties to the other. No difference between the gangsters and the politicians, they all crooks."

"I know how it be, ma'am," Shakeera said softly. "Can't find a ray of sunshine nowhere."

"That's just how life can be, girl."

"Thass my little ray of sunshine in there," Shakeera said sadly, nodding towards Sabrina's room behind her.

"I know you love her, and so do we. Dr. Schumann is doing the best thing for her, we know that. The clinic in Hawaii has the best facilities in the world, including the most advanced treatment programs for comatose patients. Nobody will question this move, and you know it's for the best."

"But what about Hoyt?" Shakeera wailed. "Sabrina is his life. How can I look him in the eye when he finds out she's gone?"

"Now you know you get paid by the Brooks Foundation," Minnie stared into her eyes. "There be some big numbers on your check, you get paid well to do what you do. They tell you this information is confidential, that's the way it is. You aren't lying to Detective Wexford. You just aren't telling him what he don't need to know. If the Brooks Foundation saw fit to tell him, you know he would already know by now."

"Is she really coming back?"

"It depends on how her treatment progresses. You just make sure you keep watch on her monitors, and make sure she is not disturbed under any circumstances. She has a long plane trip ahead of her, and she's gonna need all the rest she can get."

Miles away, Hoyt Wexford and Bob Methot were in a secluded motel room in Harrison, New Jersey. They were interviewing Carissa Fermanagh and Lori

Murphy in Carissa's second floor apartment. It was surrounded by a twelve-man squad of detectives in various hideout stations around the premises. They were well-armed and waiting for anyone who came in search of either of the women.

"So you're telling me he just up and left in the middle of the night without a word?" Hoyt grilled the women, both of who were shaken by the latest turn of events.

"I told you, he kept talking about how he couldn't leave New York for the rest of his life," Carissa wiped a tear from her eye. "We agreed with him, we don't want to leave either. We haven't done anything for the Lipkis to come after us. I know the Yakovs came here for me, but I think they were acting on their own. That's what I told Max. I think that if he went back, he went back for all of us. He wanted to end it so we could all go home."

"Stupid son of a bitch," Bob shook his head. "At least if he'd have given us a heads up we could've put a tail on him. We could've kept him from getting whacked."

"You're the police, you have Homeland Security," Lori's voice trembled. "You know he went back to Brighton, there's got to be some way you can track him down."

"He's been gone for almost two days, why didn't you say anything?" Bob said harshly. "By now he could be anywhere. They might've chopped him up, he may be in five different places by now."

"Don't you say that," Carissa wept. "Don't you say that about Max."

"C'mon, Bob," Hoyt winced at him before turning back to the women. "All right, give us anything that can help out. Anything he said that can give us an idea of what he's planning or where he's going."

"The Nightcrawler," Lori said softly. "He said he knew the Nightcrawler was still out there, and if anything happened to him, the Nightcrawler would make them pay."

"Well, that sure takes a whole lot off my chest," Bob said sarcastically, slouching back in his chair as he stared at the women.

"Let me make some calls," Hoyt rose from his seat, heading towards the door. "I just hope for Max's sake we're not too late."

Within an hour, the detectives were in the Gravesend area of Brooklyn across the street from the Lipki mansion. The New York District Attorney's office delivered a sealed indictment to a grand jury, and Organized Crime Unit squads met with Homeland Security agents in front of Lipki's home by noon. Lipki had a battery of lawyers converge on the scene, and they were arguing for their client's rights to no avail under provision of the Patriot Act. Lipki's bodyguards quietly surrendered their arms in the face of possible arrest and prosecution for possession of military-grade automatic weapons.

"I'm glad you called me in on this," Kelly Stone came over to where Hoyt and Bob stood by the parked Camry. "Maybe we don't get to send anyone to Guantanamo, but I'm pretty sure Lipki's gonna do some serious time on the RICO charge. You've closed the Russian Mafiya down in Brighton, fellows. Congratulations."

"Max Mironov's missing. The Groznys and Yuri Kurskov aren't in there. I think they're with Apollyon," Hoyt revealed.

"Who the hell is Max Mironov?"

"He's a low-level dealer who got a foot in the door with Lipki's in crowd. They thought he had something to do with the Nightcrawler stopping Apollyon at the Jackie O Reservoir. We took him and his crew in, and he snuck back out."

"Snuck out? What do you mean he snuck out?" Kelly furrowed his brow.

"Just what I said. I think it might have something to do with the Nightcrawler."

"Are you any closer to finding out where the Crawler is, or who he is?"

"No. We just need you to wait for our call. This wasn't it."

"The Nightcrawler may be the only man standing between New York City and a major catastrophe," Kelly stared into his eyes. "The Plague. The mother of all plagues. If you have any suspects, you need to bring them in. Millions of people's lives are at stake."

"We'll give you a call," Hoyt said as he and Bob got into the Camry. "You be ready."

"I'm here, aren't I?' Kelly replied.

Over his shoulder, they could see a handcuffed Stanislav Lipki being escorted to a waiting police van by the NYPD.

Months later, conspiracy theorists around the world would argue that Tryzub had coerced staff members of the Dagestan Embassy into setting up a celebrity tour of the Empire State Building. It would provide them access to the 103$^{rd}$ floor observation deck, restricted to visiting dignitaries and celebrities. Once that was arranged, it was a matter of substituting Tryzub operatives for the

Dagestani delegates. It was reported afterward they had been kidnapped during the incident. The contingent arrived at the world-famous landmark at the appointed time, and building security had no way of knowing they were escorting terrorists to the tower area until they had been rendered unconscious.

"This will truly be an unforgettable moment in history," Apollyon breathed the crisp night air at the pinnacle of the building, having changed to his combat gear after the Groznys had subdued the security guards. "Observe this great city, comrades. Within minutes, we will strike a blow that will change its history forever. Just think, for one hundred million dollars they could have spared it from its fate. The leaders of this country will forever regret not having paid the price."

"Yeah, they're gonna pay the price, all right," Yuri Kurskov chuckled as he placed the long black case upon the concrete ledge overlooking midtown Manhattan. "When this baby hits Times Square, it's gonna be the mother of all mob scenes. They're gonna go down kicking like roaches."

Max Mironov felt sick to his stomach. He had spent the last twenty-four hours in a safe house on Long Island under heavy guard. He knew that if his underwear was searched or confiscated, he was a dead man. He was given a change of clothing, and he wiped his butt with the new briefs so that they thought they were his old ones. The gambit worked, and just hours ago he had been prepped on the operation before they headed out for the rendezvous with Apollyon. Now here they were, and he knew that only a miracle would stop these maniacs. He also knew that, no matter how this ended, they would kill him so he could never testify against them.

He remembered as a teen how he and his friends would take the A Train to Manhattan and watch the people milling around Times Square. They were fascinated how so many people could crowd such a large place, how the activity seemed endless as people visited countless areas of attraction. He could envision how the throngs would panic when the rocket-launched device landed in the thoroughfare. They would know it was the Ebola bomb, and it would turn into a mob scene as people raced for shelter. Many would become hysterical in knowing they were inhaling the virus dispensed by the chemical weapon. Dozens would be trampled, and violence would be rampant as people imagined they had come to the end of their lives.

He felt as if he was hallucinating as Apollyon opened a small satchel containing the Ebola shell. Pyotr Grozny lifted the RPG-7 rocket launcher from its case, setting it on its stock as Apollyon prepared to load the projectile. He looked away and thought he was seeing things as a dark figure appeared to be standing on the ledge at the far side of the deck.

"You guys just don't give up," the Nightcrawler called over to them as they stared aghast at the vigilante. "I'm sure glad you picked a place like this. There's nowhere to go but down. You'd better give up now before someone gets hurt."

"I'm glad you showed up," Nestor Grozny stepped up behind Max, pointing his Glock-17 at the back of Mironov's head. "Now you get to see what happens to your little rat."

"*No!*" screamed the Nightcrawler.

At that, Nestor pulled the trigger, blowing a grapefruit-sized hole through Max's forehead where the hollow-point bullet exited. Max fell face first onto the covered floor, his torn skull bouncing off its surface.

"Kill him!" Apollyon roared.

The shadowy figure pulled out a gas gun as the giant fired his metal darts from his wrist launcher. The graphene on the vigilante's forearm braces kept the arrowheads from penetrating the suit though the impact was enough to paralyze the Nightcrawler's arm. It gave the gangsters time to whip out their Uzis and pour a withering hail of fire into their adversary. The crimefighter collapsed beneath the fusillade, dropping motionless into a dark corner.

"Well, that's that," Yuri snickered, ejecting the spent clip from his machine gun. "The cops'll blame it on these two after we take off."

"Hey, yeah," Pyotr turned to Apollyon. "Imagine what the jerks in this city will think. They'll think the Nightcrawler was one of the gang."

"That won't be necessary," Apollyon replied. "Throw him over the ledge. There'll be enough of a crowd outside for us to leave without anyone noticing."

The Groznys started toward the fallen figure, inwardly concerned that the urban legend might have yet another life to spare. Their fears were realized as a round object came bouncing towards them from the shadows. Apollyon was the only one to drop into a crouch as the concussion grenade erupted. The three gangsters were slammed against the wall with brutal force, nearly breaking their bones before they collapsed unconscious.

"I remember as a young man when the Russians invaded Goragorsky, the village where I lived in Chechnya," Apollyon said as the long steel blades sprung from the metal cover over his right glove. "My parents, my relatives, all my friends were arrested, many killed. There were so many just like you, who thought they could prevail against impossible odds. They fought to the last grenade, the last bullet, the last throwing knife. It was as if they wanted to die as heroes. I saw it as senseless, a foolish waste. They could have escaped, and lived to fight another day. You must have known that I was going to accomplish my mission. You knew you would die trying to stop me. Yet here we are."

"Yeah?" the Nightcrawler croaked. "Well, you'd better get going before it's too late. Better take your own advice, buster."

"You are a fool, a damned fool," Apollyon came over, looming above his fallen foe. He held the foot-long blades jutting from his fist before him as they gleamed in the moonlight. "I want to look into your eyes. I want to see your bravery in the face of death."

Apollyon reached over and yanked the vigilante's hood off. He gazed in wonderment, unable to believe what he saw.

"No!" he exclaimed. "It is impossible!"

"Yeah, well, you don't look so hot without your mask either, mister."

With that, the Nightcrawler hooked a boot behind Apollyon's right heel, shoving off the floor and slamming a left boot into the Chechen's right knee. The titanium cleats would have shattered bone upon impact, but served only to topple Apollyon backward to the ground. Yet the blow was enough to hobble the giant, who fell in a dazed heap. It gave the vigilante enough time to roll up and spring forth, tackling the daggered glove and driving it into Apollyon's thigh. The terrorist roared in agony as the Nightcrawler tumbled off to one side.

"There," the dark figure managed, still badly hurt from the automatic fire that had ravaged the tattered body armor. "That evens things up, huh?"

"I am going to throw you off this building before I launch that rocket," Apollyon hissed, barely managing to pull the daggers loose from his thigh. "Or perhaps I will let you watch and let it be the last thing you ever see."

"I'll jump off this building when I'm good and ready," the Nightcrawler pulled the black mask back on.

"Prepare yourself," Apollyon struggled to a sitting position.

Both combatants were astonished as the door to the observation deck burst open. They watched as Hoyt Wexford and Bob Methot raced onto the platform with pistols drawn. Bob pressed his gun against Apollyon's temple as Hoyt stared aghast at the Nightcrawler. He then rushed forth, kicking the weapons away from the fallen gangsters and checking their pulses.

"What the hell is that?" Bob stared at the RPG-7 on the ledge. "Is that the chemical weapon?"

"Yep, he was just getting ready to aim and fire, provided I didn't have any say in the matter," the Nightcrawler staggered to a standing position across the deck from them.

"Well, this guy isn't getting away a second time," Bob announced. With that, he pulled the trigger and blew Apollyon's brains across the ground.

"Bob!" Hoyt was stunned. "Are you outta your mind?"

"What about that one?" Bob nodded at the vigilante.

"Don't even think about it," Hoyt warned him.

"Okay, buddy, you're coming with us," Bob slowly holstered his weapon. "Everything'll be fine. You'll turn State's witness against Stanislav Lipki. No one will ever find out who you are. You'll be a national hero after this. It's over now. You'll be fine."

"Well, thanks, guys, but I gotta go," the Nightcrawler pulled up onto the ledge and rose from a crouch, standing on the edge. "I won't tell anybody about him if you don't."

"No!" Hoyt stepped forward. "We're on the 103$^{rd}$ floor! Don't do it!"

They watched in horror as the Nightcrawler dove backwards, plummeting into the darkness of midtown Manhattan far below.

# Chapter Ten

Hoyt Wexford spent the next twenty minutes staring over the precipice from which the Nightcrawler disappeared. He gazed into the inky blackness as Bob Methot prepped the scene, cuffing the Groznys and Kurzkov together at the wrists after placing a gun in Apollyon's hand. When the cops finally stormed the roof, Hoyt made his way to the stairwell and descended to the lower level. He took the elevator to the grade floor and walked in a daze back to his parked car. He gunned the engine and drove sightlessly downtown on the way to Bellevue Hospital.

He gnawed his lip, trying to keep from crying as he ran a red light. He had to reassure himself that it was not Bree who dived off that building. He remembered when he first found out that she was the Nightcrawler, watching her being thrown from a second story window by the Reaper. This was far worse. He recalled the night she was brought into Bellevue in a coma, wearing her combat gear though her mask had been removed by the EMTs. He could not imagine ever feeling worse than he did on that night, but somehow this was it. He felt as if his heart had been torn out and thrown off the Empire State Building.

If someone put a gun to his head, he could not swear that it was or wasn't Bree on that ledge. The impostor had the same voice distortion unit, having the same emphysema victim warble. The man got up from the shadows, climbed onto the ledge and did a backflip. His mind was spinning at the sight of the Nightcrawler, real or fake. He got the call, telling him to be at the building in fifteen minutes. He had no way of knowing whether it was the impostor or someone else with a distortion box. He came out onto the roof and saw a sight he never thought he'd see again. It looked just like Bree.

Now he had to see Bree lying in her bed. His sanity depended on it.

He heard the crack of thunder as a lightning bolt flashed across the cloudy black sky. It was as if a bomb went off above the hospital, but Hoyt didn't give a damn. He peeled rubber as he swerved off First Avenue, darting east on Thirtieth Street and hanging a hard right at the stop sign. His tires squealed as he veered right past the hospital into the parking lot. As he parked the Camry, huge raindrops began splattering onto the asphalt around him. He cursed and swore that it would have taken a direct meteor hit to stop him.

He was confronted by four uniformed cops as soon as he strode into the nearly-deserted lobby.

"Bob Methot said that they have choppers with spotlights searching all four sides of the Empire State Building," a beefy cop informed him. "There's no sign of the Nightcrawler. We've got a cordon along a five-block radius. He's nowhere to be found."

"How did I know that's what you were going to say?" Hoyt sneered. He had a terrible feeling that he was about to become like the biggest uniformed prick he had ever seen or heard of. "All right, you men come with me."

They bunched into the elevator and rode straight up to the neurosurgical trauma ward where Sabrina was allowed to stay. Hoyt ordered the officers to stand by at the nurses' station as he confronted Shakeera Smith at the suite entrance.

"I'm here to see Bree," he announced as she rose from her chair.

"I'm sorry, Detective Wexford, but Dr. Schumann has given strict orders that she's not to be disturbed," Shakeera visibly shrank before Hoyt's wrath.

"I just came back from stopping a gang of maniacs from dropping an Ebola bomb on Times Square," Hoyt blazed. "You can bet your life that Dr. Schumann's the least of my worries."

He nearly shoved past Shakeera as he barged into the room. The only light came through the venetian blinds as he saw the figure covered with sheets lying in the hospital bed. He noticed that all the monitors seemed normal as the patient appeared to be comfortably resting. Only he could see that she was lying on her right side. He knew that Schumann recommended that she be shifted around to avoid bedsores. Yet why was she left on one side throughout the night?

He stepped forth gingerly as if trying not to disturb her, which was absurd in considering her condition. It was almost as if he was afraid of what he might find. He approached the bed, circling around to where her long red hair was like a veil covering her face.

"Sabrina?" he half-whispered.

He reached over and placed his hand on her left shoulder. It felt cold and stiff, causing a rush of horror to race up his spine. His arm shook uncontrollably, his hand unable to release her as he pulled her toward him. He could not believe that she was dead. It was impossible. Not now.

He turned her over and stared aghast. He was unable to think, unable to speak, unable to breathe.

It was Deadwoman.

He staggered back from the bed, nearly tripping over his own feet before the reality of what he saw hit him with hurricane force. He stalked back to the entrance and grabbed Shakeera by the shoulders, his fingers as talons as the cops rushed over toward them.

"I swear, I couldn't do anything about it!" Shakeera began sobbing. "Nurse Ratched and Dr. Schumann told me they'd end my career if I disobeyed them!"

"I'll throw your ass in jail for medical fraud!" Hoyt shook her violently.

"C'mon, Hoyt," one of the cops gripped his arm. "Let her go."

"You take her downstairs," Hoyt ordered, red flashes before his eyes nearly blinding him. "Don't let her out of your sight. Get that mannequin out of my fiancé's bed and take it downtown."

"Yes sir."

Hoyt's hands continued to shake as he pulled his cell phone from his suit jacket and called Bob Methot.

"Hey, kid."

"Bree's gone."

"What?" Bob was astounded. "What do you mean? She's dead? How?"

"No, I mean she's gone, she's not here. I need you to send some black-and-whites and pick up Ratched and Schumann."

"You think they have her?"

"Maybe they know where she is, maybe not. Take them downtown for medical fraud."

"You're gonna need a warrant, kid."

"The hell I will. Get them for kidnapping. I don't give a damn how you do it, just bring them downtown."

"You got it."

Hoyt drove his fists against his temples in an effort to stop the violent throbbing. He felt as if his head was going to explode, as if his lungs were about to burst. He held his breath to keep from hyperventilating before dialing Kelly Stone.

"Geez, Hoyt, you turned your damn phone off?" Kelly demanded. "I've left a dozen messages. This stuff is all over the news. There was a shootout on top of the Empire State Building. Apollyon's dead and so is your snitch. They arrested three of Stanislav Lipki's top guys. They recovered an RPG-7 along with what they think's an Ebola canister."

"Bree's gone."

"What? Oh, good God, Hoyt. I'm so sorry."

"No," Hoyt growled. "I mean she's not at Bellevue. I need you to do me a solid. I need you to do a check on Schumann and Ratched. Dig as deep as you can."

"To hell with that. I'll send word to D.C. We'll turn this city inside out."

"Please, just do as I ask. I'm here at the hospital now, I got this. Bob's on the way to pick up Schumann and Ratched. I need to piece this together. Help me out. Please."

"Okay, Hoyt. I got your back. Just keep me in the loop. I'll do anything you want, whatever you need. Just one question."

"Yeah."

"Was it you?"

"No," Hoyt barely managed. "It was the Nightcrawler. I'll e-mail you a copy of our report."

"I owe you. This city, this country owes you."

Hoyt switched off the phone.

He stared blindly out the window, the rain pouring as if being sprayed by a garden hose against the glass. What sick mind would have thought to have put Deadwoman in Bree's bed and have Shakeera keep watch? His blood froze at the thought of Tryzub having conspired with Schumann and Ratched to kidnap Bree for whatever reason. Could they somehow have learned that Bree was the Nightcrawler? If she had been abducted by them, there was no telling what they had planned for her. After all the turmoil she had put them through, he doubted there was anything they would not do to pay her back.

He switched his phone on vibrate, and within minutes he finally got a call. It was Bob.

"Kid, I know you're not gonna wanna hear this, so brace yourself," Bob was terse. "I just got callbacks from the guys I sent out. Schumann's gone. So is Ratched."

"*What?*"

"The bastard's suite is empty. The hotel manager said he left Monday. He left no forwarding address. That bitch is gone too. She moved out of her hotel room last week. Nobody knows where they went. I have Dale Vosberg looking for them. If anyone can find them, he can."

"I want you to squeeze every rat in Brooklyn," Hoyt insisted. "Find out if anyone knows anything about either one of them. I need to know if they were connected with Tryzub or the Mafiya."

"Dammit, Hoyt, you don't think…"

"You tell me," Hoyt said before he hung up.

Suddenly he considered how he had forced Kelly Stone to move his Homeland Security agents off the ward. The thought made him sick. If he had let them keep watch over her, this could have never happened. Tryzub would have never dared made a move on her. It was an incredible blunder on his part. Maybe he could get Kelly to confiscate the hospital's videos. Someone had to have seen something. A 5'9", 140-pound woman could not simply vanish into thin air.

Fifteen minutes later, the phone buzzed again.

"I put some serious weight behind this and called up some big markers," Kelly informed him. "People went after those two like Osama Bin Laden."

"Dammit, Kelly. What have you got?"

"I don't know how to tell you this."

"Don't jerk me around, dude."

"All right," Kelly exhaled. "The whole thing's a set-up, an elaborate hoax. Schumann is Joe Reed, Ratched is Jordan Dunzell. They're stage actors from Florida. They were in some second-rate medical murder mystery, one of those restaurant shows. They hired out to some private club and left the troupe on short notice. All their paper, diplomas and resumes, were phony. It was all paid for by the same crew that reserved their hotel suites in New York."

"What crew?"

"We traced it all back to the Brooks Foundation."

"I'll get back to you."

Hoyt nearly dropped the phone as he held it limply at his side.

"Sir?"

"Yeah," Hoyt replied, turning from the cop as tears of anger rolled down his cheeks.

"The girl wants to call a lawyer."

"Let her go."

"You sure?"

"Yeah."

Suddenly he remembered the book on curare in the nightstand in Bree's room. Curare was an exotic poison used by primitive tribes. It overcame its victims by paralyzing their nervous system. If Bree had found a way to dilute or control its properties, she could use it to make herself appear dead...or comatose. It was not beyond her capacity.

*Her and Jon Aeppli.*

He paced in a semi-circle for a long minute, feeling as if he was about to go insane. He fought off a wave of nausea before finally pulling his phone up once again.

"Hello."

"Hello yourself."

"Congratulations."

"Congratulations yourself."

"Look," Jon Aeppli cleared his throat, "I was gonna call you, but everything's been insane over here. The President wants the whole staff flown to D.C. tomorrow morning. If we hadn't gotten those canisters from the reservoir, we would've never discovered the antidote."

"I don't give a damn about the antidote. Where is she?"

"She swore me to secrecy, Hoyt. I know you may never forgive me, but she's like my own daughter, you know that. She knew that after Dariya died, Tryzub would stop at nothing to get her. This was the only way she could keep them at bay while she took them down."

The line was silent for a long while.

"She saved the City, Hoyt. She saved countless lives."

He turned off the phone, realizing at last that Dariya was a double agent for Tryzub. The beautiful Dariya, Bree's kindred spirit, one of her dearest friends. Bree must have found out who Dariya was. Dariya would have tried to kill Bree. They fell out the window from Bree's office at the BCC, and Dariya broke her neck. Bree went on to take on Boko Haram and was nearly killed herself. Only she recovered.

And no one else was the wiser.

No one but the Brooks Foundation.

He broke into a wild rage and hurled his phone against the wall where it shattered into pieces. He stormed down the hall and punched the elevator button, taking the ride down to the lobby where the cops watched him expectantly. He stalked past them and shoved his way violently through the revolving door.

He rushed out into the parking lot, the rain coming down in torrents, his hair and clothing soaked within seconds. He stared wildly around the lot, gazing into heaven, asking God how and why he had been deceived so cruelly. He asked himself how he could have been so stupid. He tried to fathom how he could not have known.

"*Sabrina!*" he screamed, his voice echoing across the parking lot.

In the far corner of the lot, a figure hunkered down behind the steering wheel of the black Mercedes-Benz.

She wondered how she was going to talk her way out of this one.

Lightning Source UK Ltd.
Milton Keynes UK
UKHW041048201020
371876UK00019B/189